TANGLED

A NOVEL

TANGLED

A CHARLOTTE RIDGE MYSTERY

GWEN ENQUIST

LitPrime Solutions
21250 Hawthorne Blvd
Suite 500, Torrance, CA 90503
www.litprime.com
Phone: 1-800-981-9893

Published by LitPrime Solutions   03/08/2023

ISBN: 979-8-88703-147-7(sc)
ISBN: 979-8-88703-172-9(hc)
ISBN: 979-8-88703-148-4(e)

Library of Congress Control Number: 2023900490

To my writing group whose encouragement
turned a writing exercise into a novel

CONTENTS

ACKNOWLEDGEMENTS

I WANT TO THANK A NUMBER of people who helped bring this story to completion. To my brother, David, for his continued support and reading of the manuscript. His comments are always valuable and welcome. To Corporal John Green, RCMP, Retired, thank you for reading the manuscript and for suggestions re RCMP protocols and procedures, both needed and appreciated. And thank you to RCMP Constable Chris Bakker who filled in some knowledge gaps. Any errors or omissions are mine.

PROLOGUE

TANGLED. SO TANGLED. THE RAIN, the hut, the blackness mess me up. My insides swirl in a tangle of images: digging, so much digging. Deep hole, dig deep. Need sleep. There's no sleep here. The night is dark, so dark, dark enough to hide in. A heavy thump, the crackle of twigs under foot. Then, the emptiness of the night and the smell of new dirt. Wet, muddy dirt on my boots. Wet and dirty on the outside. Tangled on the inside.

PART 1

MISSING

CHAPTER 1

I T WAS SEVEN P.M. ON a stormy April night when a man walked into the Cranbrook, British Columbia RCMP detachment and reported to Constable Jessica Morell that his wife was missing. His coat and hat dripped icy water while his face held such distress that Jess was moved to offer a hot drink after settling him in an interview room. She had a yellow legal pad in front of her with a pen poised to record facts.

Jessica Morell, one year out of training, had straight brown hair pulled back into a neat knot at the back of her head. She was slim with narrow shoulders but an athletic build. Thick dark lashes framed deep brown eyes. Her taut demeanor said that she was eager.

"Let's start with your name," she said earnestly. She took address and telephone numbers. Her heart quickened. As a young police constable in a small town, this was exciting.

"Adam Chandler. And it's my wife who's missing.

I'm starting to get really worried. She hasn't been home since late last night." The man ignored the coffee in front of him.

"Your wife's name?"

"Aimée-Marie Chandler." He leaned over the table towards Jess. "It's not like her not to answer her phone." He took off his hat and raked his hands through his wavy brown hair that glistened with rain drops leaving it standing in spikes. He was very tall and soft around the middle, well-manicured hands. Jess figured his age at between thirty and thirty-five.

"What time last night did you last see her?" Jess recorded his answers.

"It was midnight. She got a call from the hospital and had to go out."

Jess interrupted him. "What was the problem at that time of night?"

"Aimée-Marie is a doctor. I don't know what the problem was but the hospital needed her for some reason."

"So she left." Jess scribbled notes on her pad.

"Yes." He made a distressed sweep over his hair.

"Then what happened?"

"I went to sleep and she wasn't there in the morning. That's not so unusual, that she's kept at the hospital all night. It happens. But she didn't call all day. I tried her several times from my office but she didn't pick up." He stood and began pacing. "I called the hospital and they said she left about three a.m. But I didn't know that all day and when she didn't show up or answer her phone by dinner time I got really worried." Chandler ran out of breath.

"What about her office? Was she supposed to be there during the day?"

"No, today is her closed day."

"You were at work all day yourself?"

"Yes, I had a full schedule. I had no way of knowing she hadn't gone home." He stood and began pacing.

"What do you do?"

"I'm a doctor too."

"Have you tried her friends?"

"Yes! Look you've gotta do something!" He stopped his agitated pacing and leaned on the desk invading Jess's space causing her to pull back.

"First, the friends? Who are they?"

He straightened up. "There are only a couple she might spend time with but they are a doctor and a nurse. I called them and they haven't seen her. Cathy Aikens, the nurse, was at the hospital last night on night shift and Megan Kinsey, the doctor, left the hospital as Aimée arrived. They haven't heard from her since."

"Has she ever done this before?"

"What! Disappeared?" He leaned over the desk again slapping his hands angrily on it, his face just inches from Jess's. "What are you suggesting, Constable? That she did this on purpose?" His face reddened with emotion, veins stood out in his neck. "No! She has not disappeared before! She is always in contact somehow."

Jess stood, heart rate jumping, ready for any aggressive move he might make. "Calm down, Mr., uh, Dr. Chandler." The door to the interview room opened and an officer stood in the frame.

"What's happening in here? Morell? You need me?" he said.

"I think we're good. Dr. Chandler is a bit overwrought. His wife has been missing since three a.m.," Jess explained.

"I'd be overwrought too," the officer said. He held out his hand to Chandler. "Corporal Thayer." Thayer was round in the face and chest, short grey brush-cut, Chandler taller by half a foot. Chandler shook it and calmed down enough to sit. "Let me talk to Constable Morell a minute then we'll decide how to proceed." He nodded his head to Jess gesturing for her to follow him. They closed the door behind them.

"Run their names," Thayer told her. "See if anything comes up. Maybe this is a domestic. Maybe something's happened in the past."

Jess nodded and sat at a computer. She ran the name Adam Chandler, nothing on his driver's license. He seemed clean. She ran Aimée-Marie Chandler and found her name connected to an altercation in the emergency room at the hospital. A drunk, belligerent patient shouted threats and had to be physically held back by security officers. The drunk who had numerous cuts to be stitched was Keith Rymes. The doctor doing the stitching was Aimée-Marie Chandler. RCMP had been called and Rymes arrested and taken away to sleep it off, wounds still oozing. Other than that, both seemed to be law-abiding citizens. At least it looked that way.

"Find anything?" Thayer asked looking over her shoulder.

Jess related the Rymes incident but said Chandler seemed clean.

"But, the wife must have a car. She's a doctor and has a driver's license. He hasn't mentioned the car. Where is it?" They ran Aimée-Marie Chandler's license again and found the make and model of her car. Jess made a note of the license plate number.

"Maybe she did disappear by choice. Or maybe he made her disappear," Thayer said. "Let's lean on him a bit more. I'll go in with you and see what he has to say next."

When Constable Jessica Morell and Corporal Abel Thayer re-entered the interview room, Adam Chandler was seated drumming his fingers on the table. He remained agitated but less aggressive.

"What are you going to do? You have to do something!" he challenged immediately. His face was strained and his eyes had that haunted look that worry creates.

Thayer and Jess sat down across from Chandler. "We'll do our best to find her," Thayer said. "First, tell us about life at home. Any problems or issues that could take Mrs. Chandler away?"

"Like what? What do you mean?"

"Is there anything that we should know about… about your relationship with your wife? Any problems, dissension, arguments? Any business needs that might take her away?" Thayer's eyes bore into Chandler's face across the table.

"What! No! We don't have any more problems than anyone else! You're making me out to be a suspect! Like I did something to her. You're barking up the wrong tree, Corporal. Our life was fine, fine. Do something useful like sending out squad cars to look for her." His reddened face collapsed under the strain. He covered his face in his hands and rubbed the heels of his palms into his eyes.

"Your marriage is just 'fine', Dr. Chandler? That's pretty lukewarm, I must say."

"Who are you to judge another person's marriage? You're not there day after day. I love my wife and I'm getting more worried as time goes on. We're busy people. We're fine!"

Corporal Thayer wrote some notes on the yellow pad that Jess had brought to the interview room. Chandler glared at him. "One thing that occurred to us was the location of her car. You didn't mention it. Did you check the hospital parking lot?"

Chandler's face registered shock. "Her car? God, no. I didn't think of it. I just talked to the hospital by phone." He jumped up. "I'll go right now."

"Constable Morell will go with you." Thayer stood also, giving Jess a nod. "She can check the area for evidence, of any kind."

Chandler hesitated. "Of course, that's good," he said realizing he was getting the police action he'd asked for. He put on the brimmed cap he had been wearing against the pounding rain. "I can drive," he said.

"No, Constable Morell will take a car and follow you."

"Sure. Whatever you say." As Chandler left the room, Jess looked at Thayer and raised her eyebrows.

"You know what to look for?" Thayer asked the Jess quietly. She was no longer a rookie with a training officer to guide her but Thayer had to make sure she knew what was needed.

"Sure. Any sign of a struggle. But the rain will be against us."

"Unless there's evidence inside the car. Okay, take Franks with you. If the car is there, secure it. Don't touch anything."

"Got it." Jess tagged Constable Joe Franks on the way out of the station. She filled him in on Chandler's visit by the time they got to the hospital. Chandler was out of his car and searching the parking lot when the squad car arrived.

"I've looked everywhere and the car isn't here!" Jess and Franks exited their car and covered the same ground Chandler had already. Chandler's frustration boiled over. "I told you the car isn't here!"

"We have to do our job, Dr. Chandler," Jess said evenly, "and look for any sign of a struggle. Given that the car isn't here, we'll put out a BOLO. Does the hospital have security video of the parking lot?"

"Oh, God." He ran his hand over his face then

looked up. "I don't know about cameras. C'mon, let's find security and ask."

"While we're doing this, why don't you try her cell phone again?" They walked towards the hospital, entered and asked the reception desk to page security.

The receptionist looked at Dr. Chandler with sympathy. "She isn't answering yet?" she said.

"No." His tone was flat. He punched at his phone.

A security officer arrived and told the two constables that they only had video of the emergency room entrance. Did they want to see it?

The security officer made a phone call to Head of Security and explained the situation. He was at home and would come right in.

Chandler tried his wife's cell phone several times. No answer. He tried the landline at their house. Still no answer. While they were waiting for the Head of Security, Jess asked the receptionist what time Dr. Adam Chandler called the hospital.

"You don't believe me?" Chandler's tone was shocked.

"I have to be complete in my notes," Jess replied.

Head of Security finally arrived, a middle-aged man carrying too much weight introduced himself. "Jeff Avery," he said. Jess explained what they were looking for. "Sure, right this way."

It didn't take long to isolate the right piece of tape. They saw Dr. Aimée-Marie Chandler enter the hospital through the emergency entrance and leave again, alone, three hours later at three a.m.

"Where did she go?" Chandler asked.

"That's what we have to find out," Jess said. "I'll put out the BOLO and we start talking to the staff."

Jess called Thayer and updated him. She said she would be a while and would start asking questions of staff that were at work last night.

Dr. Adam Chandler collapsed into a chair. Jess told him to go home. They would keep him informed. He protested weakly. He was clearly stunned at the unfolding evidence surrounding his wife's disappearance. Jess wondered about a wife disappearing in the middle of the night; the whys were numerous. Maybe she just left. She wondered about a husband who would *make* his wife disappear, and her car too. Wouldn't it be easier to just kill someone and leave the car? But then, the car becomes evidence and anything that forensics could find in it. Maybe he wasn't so stunned but just a good actor.

When the sun rose that morning, Adam Chandler hadn't slept yet. His stomach roiled with acid from a pot of coffee that he'd consumed over the night. The waiting was driving him crazy. He kept looking at the phone willing it to ring but anguished at what that call might tell him. His skin was practically crawling with the need to do something.

Had Aimée told Cathy or Megan anything that would be a lead? Checking the clock it was almost time for Cathy to come home from night shift. Sitting here accomplished nothing. He grabbed his jacket and keys and left.

As he reached the Aikens's house he noticed that Kevin's truck was still in the drive. He hadn't left for work yet. Cathy's car was there. Adrenaline driving him, he knocked with force. Cathy, still in uniform, answered the door.

"Adam, what's happening?" Anxiety played across her face. "Any news?"

"No, but I can't believe you know nothing. You are her closest friend. You must know something that explains this." He elbowed his way into the hallway.

"I already told you. And I told the police last night. She didn't say anything. As far as I know she had no plans."

Kevin Aikens appeared in the kitchen doorway toweling his hair from a shower. He was dressed in jeans and a white T-shirt, a glowing cigarette already in his mouth. Two young boys sat at a breakfast table behind him, eating cereal. "What's happening?" he said. The boys looked up with interest.

"There's still no word," Cathy answered. "Have you found her car?"

"No, it wasn't at the hospital."

"What about on the road home? Maybe she ran off the road," Kevin said. By now the boys were standing in the doorway with him.

Adam considered this. "I should have looked. I didn't look." He turned to the door.

"I'll go with you," Kevin said pulling on the cigarette.

"No, I'll do it," Adam said sternly.

"Let Kevin help, Adam. Of course, he'll help." Cathy's face was deeply lined with worry.

"Can we help?' one of the boys asked hopefully.

"No. Eat your cereal," Cathy Aikens said.

Adam exited the house and was on the sidewalk when Kevin caught up with him, reached for Adam's arm.

"Let me do this," Kevin said.

Adam shook off his hand. "I don't want your help," he said getting in the car.

Kevin opened the passenger door. "Not even if Aimée's life hangs in the balance? You hate me that much?" He waited. "I'll just go in my own truck if I can't come with you."

Adam said nothing but ground his jaw as Kevin stamped the cigarette out and climbed into the car; he revved the engine and took off as Cathy watched the tense exchange from the window.

CHAPTER 2

Aimée-Marie Chandler was still missing a day later. The tension level at the RCMP detachment ramped up as the hours passed. The feeling that something terrible had happened to her shadowed everything they did. Jess and Joe Franks finished interviewing the staff at the hospital that were working that night and got names from the duty schedule of others on days off. No one told them anything helpful. As far as anyone knew, Dr. Chandler had finished with her patient around three a.m. and was heading home. Everyone expressed shock that she was missing.

Staff Sergeant Sturgis ordered a canvass of her neighbourhood. Neighbours were asked about any unusual activity at the Chandler house around the time of the doctor's disappearance. Could anyone lend any light on the couple and their home life? All reports spoke kindly about the couple and expressed shock that "that lovely Dr. Aimée" was missing.

A day passed and then another. Jess, now on daytime hours, sat in front of a computer checking the woman's credit card and cell phone records. There had been no activity on any of it. And Aimée-Marie Chandler had not returned home from some spur-of-the-moment mini-vacation. She had just disappeared without a trace.

"We have to look closer at the husband," Staff Sergeant Sturgis told Jess. "Today, I want you to talk to her friends, those two women he mentioned. Before, we just asked them about when they saw Chandler last, any plans she had. Now we have to press them. Get a temperature on the marriage. They might give us some clues as to their relationship, things she would confide to a close friend and that her husband wouldn't tell us. Arguments, money problems, any tensions. That sort of thing."

"Got it," Jess said. She went back to the notes that she'd taken when Dr. Chandler came in to report his wife missing. One friend, Megan Kinsey, was a doctor. She looked up her office phone number to check on her whereabouts. Her receptionist said she was still at the hospital but had office hours starting at one o'clock. Jess told her she would be in just before one o'clock to talk to the doctor.

With her next call to the hospital she learned that Cathy Aikens, RN, was just getting off duty. When she pressed Human Resources she got the home address and phone number. She would visit her at home. It was only nine a.m.; she would probably still be there.

Jess found the address in a middle-class neighbourhood where early shrubs had bloomed and grass was greening. The Aikens' residence was a modest two-story stucco house with a basketball hoop over the carport which contained a truck with a logo on the door. Aikens was a contractor with his own business. Jess parked on the street and locked the squad car.

Cathy Aikens answered the door in a pink housecoat. She was a petite woman whose brown hair was clipped loosely on the top of her head. She wore a puzzled, anxious look when she saw the uniform.

"You've found her? Has something happened?"

"Ms. Aikens, I'd like to talk to you some more about Dr. Chandler. May I come in?"

"Which Dr. Chandler?" she asked, her face pulled into a frown.

"Your friend, Aimée-Marie. And Dr. Adam Chandler, too. It might help us. May I come in?"

Cathy Aikens stepped away from the doorway and turned into the living room on the right. Jess noticed the casual lived-in look of the place; ashtrays with butts, pillows thrown around. Nothing was perfect. She faced Jess with a determined stance. "Well? What have you got?"

"We're still searching for her, Ms. Aikens. I'm hoping you can give me more background information that we could work with."

"I told you when I saw her and what she was doing. I was on shift that night she came into the hospital.

What more can I do?" She motioned Jess to sit on the sofa and Aikens sat as well.

"We haven't found any action on her credit cards or cell phone after that midnight call. Has she ever gone away before for a few days, either telling people or not?"

"You mean just take off?" Aikens seemed horrified. "She's a doctor. She has responsibilities. She would never just take off."

"Then, has she ever taken some days by herself having arranged coverage with colleagues?"

Aikens hesitated and cocked her head. "You think she went away, don't you? We're all worried sick she might be hurt, or kidnapped, dead even, and you think it's just a holiday."

"We don't think any one thing, Ms. Aikens. We're exploring all possibilities. I understand your concern for your friend but we need more information."

Cathy Aikens seemed to deflate. Her eyes welled. "You need to find her," she said softly.

"We're doing our best. Now, did she ever go away by herself?"

Another hesitation. "Sometimes she feels she needs a break. Too many stresses to deal with."

"Like what?"

"She's a doctor. What do you expect? People are sick and dying and she's there." Cathy gulped back a sob. "It's hard."

"Anything else? One of the biggest stressors for most people is family. There always seem to be issues. What about the Chandlers? Was everything smooth there?"

Cathy Aikens sighed deeply, hesitated. "I've been thinking about this a lot, wondering if I should say anything. But she's been gone too long without word. This is hard to say… but… she and Adam have had some rough patches in the last year. She told me the only thing she could think might fix it was a break for them."

"So she left him."

"Only for a week. She went to a retreat on the Sunshine Coast."

"Did she tell you any particular thing was going on?"

Aikens took a breath. "She mentioned differences they were having. Like, she wanted to move to a larger centre, Kelowna or Vernon. She liked Kelowna. He wanted to stay here for the slower pace and the outdoor lifestyle."

"Did they argue?"

"She told me they sometimes did."

"Did it ever get heated? Heated enough for abuse, violence?"

A figure appeared in the kitchen doorway, a medium build man in a housecoat and coffee cup in his hand. "What's going on?" he said. "Did they find Aimée?"

Cathy crossed the room to stand by her husband. "No. They're just asking more questions. This is my husband, Kevin."

"You were about to tell me about tensions in the marriage," Jess prodded.

"Look, I don't feel right talking about this. Aimée told me things in confidence." She stood, now twisting the ring on her left hand.

"This could be a life and death situation. I need context about their marriage, Ms. Aikens. It can only help us refine our investigation. How rough was the rough patch? Have you ever known Dr. Chandler to be physically abusive to his wife?"

She sighed. "Okay. She told me… she hit him once, an opened-handed slap, pushed him against a railing on their stairway. I was shocked. I've never seen her agitated like that even when something was going wrong with a patient. That wasn't really her style." She stared defiantly. "Something must have really provoked her. She was remorseful about it."

"So she has a temper. Did she say how he took that?"

"She said he grabbed her arms, screamed in frustration and stormed out. That time she was gone when he got home, gone for three days. She called Dr. Kinsey who covered for her."

"And when she got home?"

"Things had settled down. They've been getting along okay."

"When did this happen?"

"About four months ago. But, they're fine now," she rushed to say. "He's really worried about her."

"But, that wasn't the only time," Jess prompted. "Do you happen to know the name of the retreat she used on the Sunshine Coast?" Cathy Aikens looked at her quizzically. "I just have to check facts."

Cathy said she didn't know and began moving towards the front door, clearly ready to end the questioning. "You have to find her, Officer. She's my best friend."

"We're working on it, ma'am." She nodded at the husband as she left.

Jess sat in the squad car outside the Aikens house for several minutes thinking over the conversation. Aimée-Marie Chandler had a temper and there could have been a fight. Adam Chandler could have retaliated, too hard, and killed her. It was possible. It would have to have happened after Aimée got back from the hospital. How possible is that? Two doctors who should be sleeping getting into it after three a.m. Or… sometime during the next day when Chandler said he was trying to reach her. There were a lot of hours there. They only had his report about that day's events. They needed to check his cell phone history.

Maybe because the marriage was rocky, she was seeing someone else. Or he was. The possibilities were growing. She started the car and headed back to the barn, the colloquial name the members give to their detachment premises. She wanted to find which retreat Aimée-Marie had gone to. Perhaps they could tell her something about that time period.

Back at the detachment she told Staff Sergeant Sturgis about the interview with Cathy Aikens. "So, he lied to us. Things weren't 'fine'." Discord in the marriage was a big new line of enquiry, he said, and to carry on with checking Dr. Adam's cell phone history and finding which retreat Aimée-Marie went to. "Also, check with his office about his schedule that day. When did other people actually see him?"

She dug into the work, looked up retreats on the Sunshine Coast, called them all. No one had seen Dr. Aimée Chandler for almost a year. At the Dancing Willow Yoga and Spa Retreat on Highway 101 north of Sechelt she was told Aimée-Marie Chandler used to be there quite regularly but not recently. They looked back in their records. The last time was over a year ago.

So where did the doctor go to when she left town? And with whom? She had lied to her best friend about her whereabouts. She had something to hide.

There was still no activity on the missing doctor's credit cards. She hadn't checked into a hotel or retreat. Hadn't eaten in a restaurant, unless paying cash for everything. Not likely. Adam Chandler's cell phone history showed multiple calls to his wife's number the day she went missing. That only proves he knows how to cover his tracks, she thought. Or, he's telling the truth.

When one o'clock approached she closed the window on the computer and drove to Dr. Kinsey's office. Her office was part of a medical clinic in a long low building that housed twelve doctors. She let the receptionist know she wanted to see Dr. Kinsey before she started her afternoon hours. The receptionist, grey-haired and fiftyish, acted like this would throw the whole afternoon's schedule, but huffily relented. An aide showed her to Dr. Kinsey's office where she waited five minutes until the doctor arrived.

Megan Kinsey was tall with short-cropped dark

hair and a round face that glowed with the hormones of her obvious pregnancy. A blue sweater covered the baby bump and was topped with a white lab coat.

"Officer," she said extending her hand, not at all unsettled by this interruption to her day. "Megan Kinsey. How can I help you?"

"Constable Morell. I'm investigating the disappearance of your friend, Aimée-Marie Chandler."

"I've already talked to someone, a sergeant, I believe. Have you made any progress? This is so unsettling."

"We're trying to get a picture of Dr. Chandler's life, things that might influence other events in her life. Like tensions, stresses, money problems, marriage problems. What can you tell me about anything like that?"

The doctor sat behind her desk, thinking a moment about the question.

"Work is always a stress. Sometimes Aimée said she had to get away for a while. Even though she loved her work, she took more time off than any other doctor I know. You know, now that I'm saying this out loud, I've had concerns about her. I've thought that maybe she shouldn't be a family doctor, couldn't cope with all it takes to do the job."

"Are you saying she was unstable?"

"Not really, more fragile than unstable. She shouldn't have been carrying a whole practice. It's pretty daunting. I talked to her about cutting back hours and patients. She wasn't ready to do that, she said."

"Do you know of any stresses in the marriage that might have added to that?"

"Marriage? You want to know about her marriage?" Megan Kinsey sat up straight.

"It's routine, doctor, to get a picture of the person's whole life. It gives context. Is there anything you can tell me? Do she and her husband argue?"

"Adam is a good husband, a good partner. Since I've been pregnant she talked a bit about doing that, too. Things are going well for them. She wondered if it was the right time."

"You didn't really answer my question. Have you ever seen any discord in their marriage? Any signs of anger, of physical abuse?"

"You think Adam hit her? Killed her? Oh, no, no. You're far off the mark there. Aimée goes away on retreats sometimes. But that's her fragile nature. She needs the down time."

"So you've never seen any signs that she's been hit, no bruising, marks, anything like that?"

"As I've said, you're way off the mark." Her voice was tight as she stood. "Now, I must get on with my office hours."

"One more thing. If Aimée was fragile, is there any possibility she would commit suicide?"

Shock appeared on Dr. Megan's face. "No! How could you suggest such a thing? None at all. I told you. They were, are, in a good place. Now, I must get on."

Jess left with more questions than answers. If Aimée-Marie was fragile and not coping well with her practice, why did she want to move to a larger centre where the pressure could, possibly, be greater? Why wasn't it possible that she would commit suicide? Why didn't Dr. Megan mention the arguments in the marriage? Where had Aimée gone when she took off for a few days?

Sturgis would call Adam Chandler back for another interview. Jess wanted to sit in.

CHAPTER 3

A CANOE WITH PADDLES LEANED AGAINST the wall in the hallway next to Jess's apartment door. She'd asked the neighbor if she could leave it there. No one in the four-plex seemed to mind. Inside, the small apartment was crowded with camping gear, a tent, hiking backpack, cooking necessities, and lanterns. Jess was an outdoor enthusiast with a special liking for camping and canoeing trips. They relaxed her which, in the end, rejuvenated her. She wasn't a fan of large cities or traffic. The assignment to the Cranbrook detachment was a perfect fit.

She was packing her hiking gear and a lunch when she glanced out the window and saw Todd Henley standing on the sidewalk in front of her building. He looked up, saw her and waved. She gave a curious wave back. He made for the doorway and she heard him on the stairs.

"I'm glad you're home. I…" He hadn't been to Jess's place before and was astonished at the clutter of boxes and equipment in her small space.

"I know," she said, "it's like a rat's nest. I need a larger place but this is all that was available."

"What is it all?"

"Outdoor gear. Camping, hiking, canoeing. I love the life. I'm just packing for a short hike before work. Want to come?"

"Yeah. That sounds great. But I need to change my shoes and grab a jacket."

"I'll wait for you. Today I am doing a short hike on the Tanglefoot/Maus trail to Tanglefoot Lake. Taking lunch. Pack something to eat, drink and meet me back here in half an hour. I've got the First Aid stuff, matches, that sort of thing. Wear good shoes that will withstand water."

As Todd left, Jess wondered why she had been so quick to invite him. She loved solitary hikes into nature that enriched her spirit and felt some regret that today's walk would require her to be social. Todd was a colleague, a fellow constable. It wasn't Todd, himself, that bothered her, although he did stand too close sometimes. His tall presence seemed to hover over her, seemed to breath down her neck, causing her to shift away from him. Or maybe she was being too sensitive. Well, what harm can a walk in the country do?

The hike was a four hour return walk that encompassed meadows, rocky trails, Mause Creek, with the half-way point at Tanglefoot Lake. She set the pace not wanting Todd's presence to slow her down. He liked to talk which broke the solitude, but they encountered so many other day-trippers that the outing as a solitary adventure wasn't going to happen. She relaxed into his company. She could tell he wasn't very experienced at hiking, although he threw himself into it today, and they ended by talking about the best equipment for outdoor activities.

Todd tried to get personal, opening the conversation to special people in her life, but she didn't bite. Not that there was anyone special. She just felt private about it and didn't want to encourage Todd's interest by admitting to being available.

Lunch by the lake was wonderful. "This is what keeps me sane," Jess said.

"What's that?"

"Nature, raw nature, nothing sculptured by man."

"So even that little bridge that we crossed was an affront to you?" He was teasing.

She smiled. "Tease if you want to but I think a lot of the troubles of our society stem from dense living, not being connected to nature. We are animals, after all. We're not meant to live in cities and high-rises."

"More like caves and cedar shelters?" He pulled at the grass and put a blade in his mouth.

"Now you've got the picture." She laughed. "You look horrified."

He laughed too. "I like mod-cons, as they say."

"Yeah, washing clothes on a rock doesn't have a lot of appeal. So I guess I'm a hypocrite."

"Only in the nicest way."

"Well, living in a place like Cranbrook satisfies some of my primordial needs."

He looked at her and couldn't tell if she was flirting. She certainly sounded like she was flirting.

"We've got to start back," she said as she put away lunch debris.

"It's been a wonderful start to the day. Beats lazing around the apartment for hours before a shift."

"You can't get this in the city, can you?" She looked around the lush area, the sun-kissed blue lake that rippled in a light breeze. Birds and butterflies flitted between flowers. It filled her up and renewed her spirit.

"Rare to find, for sure. Thanks for asking me."

She laid back again, hands behind her head, and drank nature's beauty. "I really have to get out of that crappy apartment. Find a house to rent or something."

"I could help you look," Todd offered.

"Uhmm, thanks," she said, then sat up. "We need to start back to have some time before work." She packed the remnants of lunch and started out, picking up the pace as they went.

Todd hadn't been a bad companion, but, on the way back it occurred to her to wonder why Todd had come to her building in the first place. Why was he on her street this morning looking up at her apartment? What was that about?

Later that day at work, Jess felt Todd looking at her

across the office watching her work. He'd been a fun companion on the hike never crossing any line too personal. He'd had a modest amount of outdoor experience and wasn't an anchor around her waist, although the Tanglefoot/Maus hike was easy and pleasant with flowering meadows so his skills weren't tested.

He hadn't been clear about why he was on her street looking at her building. He glossed over it as an exercise, said he was just getting to know the town, registering street names and businesses so he knew where things were. Jess found it a weak response as all officers and squad cars had a GPS.

She wasn't eager to figure out the puzzle that was Todd Henley. She was stuck with him at work but would be more careful about involving Todd in her free time. She'd search for a house on her own. She looked up and found Todd looking back. He quickly ducked his head.

She heaved a breath and went back to the file on the monitor. The Chandler file. She read everything they had so far going over everything as if for the first time. One omission caught her attention. They knew that Keith Rymes had once had an altercation with Dr. Aimée in the ER but what about other patients? She immediately phoned the ER and spoke with the manager.

"Yes, we're interested in names of any patients or family members that have had an angry exchange with Aimée-Marie Chandler. Can you supply that?"

"There are rules for confidentiality here, Officer.

But, I can probably help. I can't tell you anything about why they were in the ER, you understand."

"Yes, I understand. But, altercations are a security issue and that's all I want to know about."

"Can this wait until tomorrow. It's quitting time but I'll make up a list. I'll leave it with the head nurse in the ER. You can pick it up anytime."

Good. It might open up another line of inquiry. She let Sturgis know what she had done and he approved.

After dinner time, at Sturgis's request, Adam Chandler arrived at the station. Constable Jessica Morell waved Dr. Adam Chandler into an interview room. Judging by his appearance, the last few days had been hard on him. His grey face needed shaving; bags under his eyes testified to poor sleep and the wrinkled mass of clothing might have been the same ones he'd worn when he first came to the detachment for help.

"Thank you for coming in, Dr. Chandler," Staff Sergeant Sturgis said. "I appreciate you must be busy."

"I'm not working. I'm just waiting." He jumped right in. "Do you have news? Anything? I can't take much more of this." He sat heavily into a hard chair.

"We have some more questions, Dr. Chandler," Staff Sergeant Sturgis said.

"Questions! How is that going to help? You need people searching, not questions!"

"Doctor, we need some leads on where to look and we're hoping you can give those to us." Sturgis was solicitous, careful to let Chandler know he was on his side.

Chandler relaxed a little, no longer on the edge of his chair. "Okay, what specifically?"

Jess put a yellow pad in her lap for notes as Sturgis took the lead.

"We know from your wife's friends that she sometimes went to a retreat on the Sunshine Coast. But they haven't seen her in a year. Where else might she go?"

"I don't know. Once she said she went to Kelowna but I have no idea where she stayed."

"You didn't know where your wife was for days at a time?"

"Of course, I did. I mean we talked on the phone every day. It's not like she was AWOL for God's sake."

"But you can't confirm the name of the retreat."

"No, not now. I don't know. It was a while ago. A few months." He was rattled, washing his face with his hands. "She went to a medical conference in Kelowna, too. But she was at a hotel then."

"Name of the hotel?"

Jess noted the name.

"Doctor, one of your wife's friends said she was fragile. Does that description match what you know about her?"

Chandler took a breath. "I wouldn't call her fragile. On occasion she needs to be away, out of the practice for a rest. It, the practice, can be grueling. I handle the physical demands of a practice, long hours and lack of sleep, better than she does. But she recoups on these retreats and comes back ready for the challenge again.

She loves her work." He took another breath. "Look, where is this getting us?"

"Someone also said your wife has a temper, that she lashed out at you, physically. What can you tell me about that?"

Chandler clearly wasn't expecting that and sat up startled. "You think there's violence between us? Is that what you're saying?"

"She told someone she hit you. Is it not true?" Sturgis's tone was earnest.

Chandler was silent. "That has nothing to do with anything." More silence.

"But...," Sturgis said.

"There was one night... she came unraveled. She'd lost a patient, a child, and it hit her hard."

"Then she hit you and you hit her back."

"No, no! She hit me but she was flailing. She didn't mean it."

"When someone hits you there is an impulse to hit back," Sturgis persisted.

"Well, I didn't," he ground out. "I took her wrists and held them, then I turned around and left her on her own in the house for a while."

"You think it's a good idea to leave someone who is distressed?"

"You don't understand. Aimée needs alone time. She's always been like that."

"Then what makes you think anything different is happening now?"

"Because I can't reach her by phone! She's been out

of contact for days! She left her office hours uncovered. She's never done that!" He jumped up. "You don't seem to understand that this is seriously different. You don't… oh, why am I talking to you? Why don't you do something, like, like… put out an appeal for information. Isn't it time to go to the media, ask people if they have seen her? Put her picture on the news."

Sturgis was thoughtful. "Okay, it is time for that. If that's the route you want to go, I can back that. But, be prepared for crank calls, media attention that you don't want. But, hopefully, it will bring information we're just not getting now." He stood. "I'll notify the media. Dr. Chandler, do you want to make a personal appeal?"

"Yes, yes, of course I'll do it." His face was eager, hopeful.

"Okay, I'll call you when we're ready."

Sturgis stared after Chandler as he left. "This doesn't mean he's not good for it," he said. Jess considered the man and his anguish, thought of the possibility of him killing Aimée-Marie and doubted that that had happened. Or was he snowing them all? Was he a good actor, but, not good enough to fool Sturgis? Perhaps she was just naïve when it came to reading people. Appearances cannot be trusted, she told herself. That was a grim rule of thumb. She didn't want to go there.

Back in the squad room, Sturgis and Thayer were putting together some comments for the press. Henley looked over their shoulders adding affirmative noises as they worked. Jess sat at her desk wondering about the next move.

CHAPTER 4

"MEGAN, I KNOW I'VE ALREADY asked what you know, but, I'm jumping out of my skin. I have to do more, something. You were a best friend to Aimée. Surely she confided things. Surely, you can tell me something." Adam Chandler's strained voice vibrated on the end of the line.

"Adam." She was at a loss for words. Adam sounded so distraught. His agitation level had reached new heights in the last few days. "Adam, she didn't ask me to cover if that's what you're insinuating."

"I'm not insinuating anything. It's just... I noticed her travel case is missing, the one she keeps stocked for her out-of-town trips."

"Well, what can I tell you? She didn't ask me to cover. Look, maybe talk to Cathy, see if she knows anything. Doesn't the missing bag give you hope? I mean, if there were plans..."

"She might not be injured, or dead. Yeah, I get that,

but… what if… what if she were leaving me? What if that's what it means? Did she give you any indication of another man? Tell me, Megan."

"Talk to Cathy," she said and punched off the phone.

"You know something, Megan! You know something!" he yelled. She was gone.

He quickly dialed Cathy Aikens. She picked up out of breath.

"Adam, I just finished my shift. Just walked in," She was breathless. "Is there news? What's happening?"

"What's happening is that you know something! You're keeping something from me. Aimée's travel bag is missing. Where is she, Cathy?" He couldn't check his anger.

"I don't know where she is, honest."

"But you know she's alive, right? You know something."

"I don't know anything that you don't."

"You're lying! You and Megan are lying to me!"

"I don't have to listen to this." The line went dead.

Adam jammed at the buttons on the phone and threw it onto the sofa. He threw himself beside it. Aimée wouldn't leave without making arrangements for her patients. He was sure of that. It would be unethical and irresponsible. Aimée was neither. He could hardly think about her leaving him. His heart hurt just considering it. That brief, whatever it was, with Kevin Aikens was over, he was sure. If her friends knew about another man, if she was planning it, it wasn't happening right now. It wouldn't happen like this.

The phone rang beside him. Staff Sergeant Sturgis's name declared that he wanted to see him. Oh, God. More harassment or bad news. He really couldn't handle either one.

It was just then that the first egg thrown at his house splattered on the window.

Flo Nilsson opened the General Store in Charlotte Ridge at eight a.m. as her routine. Going in the back door she didn't see Carl Thurlow on the front porch until she unlocked the front door. He was wet, his clothes giving off the pungent odour of the dank outdoors. His cheeks sprouted stubble that was past fashionable. Eyes sunken in his head, he wiped his nose with his sleeve.

"Carl! What in God's name! You look like you've been out all night. Are you sleeping up on the ridge again?" She shepherded him to the bathroom at the back of the store where she kept a supply of towels and soap because Carl often slept rough and Flo couldn't stand to see him suffer. She assisted Carl out of his muddy, rain-soaked coat and told him to dry himself off.

Carl, silent until now, said "I'm cold, cold." His body trembled.

"Yeah, I know. We have to get you home and warmed up." She left Carl to go to the phone and call Zander. "Come as soon as you can. He needs to get in a hot shower and some dry clothes. Where's that brother of his? Where's Bobby?"

"Probably sleeping one off," Zander said. Flo closed the phone.

"He dug a big hole," Carl said.

"Who dug a hole?" Flo vigorously rubbed at Carl's wet hair with a towel.

"Somebody dug a hole." He was bobbing his head as Flo toweled him.

"Somebody's always digging a hole, especially in the spring, for a garden, you know."

"A garden hole," Carl said nodding. "To plant potatoes. A big hole to hide sin and plant potatoes."

"What are you going on about sin for? Who's filling your head with nonsense like that?" She gave him a drink of water. "You're one of God's special people. There's no sin in you," she said. "Now, here's Zander and he'll take you home. Get in a nice hot shower. Zander will stay with you if Bobby's not there. Okay? Zan, make sure he eats, too."

"Right, Gran. Let's go, Carl. I'm ready for coffee and toast. You can spoon out the jam."

"Staff Sergeant," Jess said. "Should Chandler bring in something for a DNA profile of his wife? As things unfold we might need it." She might be dead at the hand of an unknown suspect, body to be found later.

Sturgis looked up from his work. "Yes. Good. Call him and tell him to bring something to the press conference."

She waited a few minutes to let Chandler get home, then called.

After identifying herself she asked Chandler to bring some items that might have Aimée-Marie's DNA on them. He went immediately into panic mode.

"There's a body isn't there! Where'd you find her?" Jess heard him moan.

"No, Doctor, no body. Nothing's changed since you were here. We just want the sample on file… for the future."

"You've lost hope then. You don't think we'll find her." It was a flat statement.

"That's not so either. This is routine. We're just rounding out our file on her. Please don't despair, sir. This has no added meaning." She could picture him running his hand through his hair. It was a distinctive gesture of his. An endearing gesture that would be a tell if he ever tried to disguise himself.

Jess checked herself. She had to stop feeling so soft towards him. He could be a murderer. "Sir, please bring the items when you come for the press briefing at… one moment. Staff Sergeant Sturgis is talking." She covered the phone with her hand. "The press has been told to gather at three p.m. The message and her picture will make the evening news."

"Thank you. I'll be there." He rang off.

As Jess worked on the list of people involved in security issues with Aimée Chandler at the hospital, she felt eyes on her. She looked up and found Todd Henley staring at her. She held his gaze. He stood, crossed the room and hitched a hip on the side of her desk.

"This is a far cry from B and Es, isn't it? Or rear-enders in a parking lot," he said.

"It's a puzzle. One I'm thoroughly enjoying. If that's appropriate when someone might be murdered."

"It's why we all become RCMP. The big stuff. Then we land in a small town and push papers for domestics and burglary of a pawn shop."

"You sound almost bitter," Jess said cocking her head.

"Nope. Not when I get to work alongside you." He smiled a wicked grin.

"I could almost arrest you for that smile, it's so lecherous."

"Ha, ha. Just kidding, Jess. Just wondered if you want to catch some supper after shift. I'll behave. Promise. You've seen the extent of my lechery. C'mon. Keep me company."

Ever since their hike together, Jess had noticed Todd. He was dark, handsome and self-contained, easy to work beside. He had one of those faces that seemed in perfect symmetry. His whole manner was restrained with never a hint of stepping over any personal line. Her determined pull-back from him was softening. After a thoughtful moment, Jess said yes.

They sat over fish and chips at The Barn Door, everyone's favourite bistro. They'd never been together in a social way like this before and the talk was, at first, awkward, centering on work, until Jess called a halt.

They were in civvies but known to the town as cops. She didn't want shop talk to become town gossip. "Time to change the subject," Jess said.

"Right," Todd agreed. They waited, fooled with their napkins. "Do you like Cranbrook?" Todd asked. They chuckled together at the lame opening.

"I'm an outdoors person, you know that; I like to be close to nature and everything that allows for leisure," she said honestly.

"Like sleeping in a damp sleeping bag while mosquitos dive-bomb your head?" The tease wasn't subtle.

"Yeah, like that." And they both laughed.

Todd's eyes held hers. "I'm going to like getting to know you," he said.

"Someone threw an egg at my house!" Adam Chandler sat in an RCMP interview room, red-faced and outraged at the recent targeting of his house. "It's your fault," he raged at Sturgis, pointing his finger. "You keep pulling me in here and people are starting to talk, to act out. I don't deserve this," he finished as he slumped in his chair.

"Look, Dr. Chandler," Sturgis said all reasonable, "we're doing everything we can to find your wife and you're a big part of that. We've put her picture out to the media with an appeal for information. The only way we're going to get anywhere is if you help us and the public comes across with info." He paused. "Any idea who egged your house?"

"No," he said weakly. "Someone ran down the street. I'd say a young person by the way he moved."

Jess sat silently in the room, notebook in her lap, watching the doctor's face and demeanor. She wasn't looking forward to Sturgis's interrogation. Chandler was anguished enough. Perhaps he deserved to be.

"A young male, then," Sturgis stated.

"As far as I could tell." Chandler ran a hand over his face.

Sturgis sat down opposite Chandler. "Okay, Doctor, this is where we're at. We've contacted any retreats that your wife has attended that we are aware of. She isn't at any of them nor has she been for about a year. Which raises the question, if she's been away in the last year, and you say she has been, where was she? Where did she go? And maybe, more to the point, who was she with and where?"

"Who? You mean you think she went with someone?" Emotions played across his face, shock and dismay followed by anger. "Are you suggesting she was with another man?"

"That's one conclusion. Does any of this make some sense to you? Has there been anything that might lead you to believe she was having an affair, Doctor?"

Chandler sat there with his mouth open, the officer's statement ringing so true with the conversations he just had with Megan and Cathy and what he knew about

Kevin. He didn't want to think like this. He didn't want that possibility to be part of public knowledge.

"Doctor, if this is possible, there are a couple of conclusions we could reach. One, she took off with her lover," Chandler's jaw tightened, "or you found out about the affair and confronted her. It became heated, physical and she ended up dead."

"You think I killed her! No! No! I would never, never. That is so wrong."

"Do you see, Doctor, why we've come to this place? The reality is that these situations almost always involve a family member. And you're number one on the hit parade."

He let that sink in. Chandler just sat there, not squirming as Sturgis would expect if he had struck a nerve. Sturgis waited for him to speak.

"You don't know that she's dead. I. Did. Not. Kill. My. Wife," Chandler said and clamped his jaw shut.

"And you've told us, even emphasized that your wife would never leave her patients without coverage. So… tell us again how 'fine' your marriage is. Tell us about the time she hit you. Tell us there is no violence in your marriage." Sturgis pounded his fist on the desk, stood to get in Chandler's face.

"You can't intimidate me. I want a lawyer," Chandler said. He crossed his arms, mouth in a grim line, and was done.

Sturgis and Jess got up and left him alone. Back in the squad room Sturgis gave Jess directions. "I want to know about the family finances. Who has what money and who's insured for how much money. Get on it. Let him sit there for a while to sweat, then let him go."

Jess got busy, left as many phone messages as she could to get the information Sturgis asked for. While waiting on the bank and insurance companies, she decided to retrace some steps. She took one of the copies of Aimée-Marie's picture that Chandler had provided. With picture in hand she set out for the yoga studio Aimée-Marie used. A class was in session. The yoga instructor stopped and greeted Jess with the distress of a best friend. Under her blue leotard and tights she was taut and lithe with golden hair in a braid.

"Oh, oh, I can't believe anything has happened to Aimée. She is the nicest, sweetest person. Everyone loves her." A name tag proclaimed her to be Natasha.

"You sound quite close to her."

"Well, you know, when a group of women work out together, well, we talk sometimes. Aimée was, oh dear, is, I mean, *is* so nice to us all. She always gives me a handsome tip at Christmas and, once, when she heard it was my birthday, she treated me to lunch. She's so special." Natasha's eyes filled and she blinked hard to stem the tears.

"I was wondering if she ever confided in you or any of the other people here. Like where she goes on her mini-vacations or who she spends time with."

"Other than her times here, I didn't see her. She was so busy, you know. But she always took time for yoga."

"You might know about the retreats she used when she went out of town."

"I know a couple." She gave the names to Jess as she wrote them in her notebook.

"Is there anybody here right now that knows Dr. Chandler, that I could talk to?"

Natasha looked around. She shook her head. "Not right now. This is a different group. But... once she met a man when she went out the door. He was friendly with her, you know, arm-around-the-shoulder friendly."

"Had you seen him before?"

She thought a moment. "Maybe twice."

"Can you describe him?"

"Oh, sort of medium build, forty-five to fifty. Not Dr. Chandler, not her husband. I know who he is. There was nothing too memorable about him. I thought it might be a brother or something."

"When was this, do you remember?"

"Oh, a few months ago, I'd say."

"Thank you, Natasha. Every bit of information is a help."

"Oh, find her soon, please."

"We are doing our best."

Back in the car, Jess considered her next move. So there might be another man. Seems that Sturgis was leaning in the right direction.

Nobody had looked through the doctor's office, her desk, for any information that might be there. She headed to the medical building.

She hit a roadblock at the reception desk. This clinic had offices for three doctors and the receptionist was on the phone as Jess entered. Finally free, she told Jess,

"You need to talk to the manager but I'll bet you need a court order because of the confidential information that might be there." She called the manager who told Jess the same thing. "Certainly you can't go through her computer without a court order."

"But, we're not going to charge her with a crime. It's to help find her."

"Sorry." The manager said. "I'd like to help but, I can't allow access." She stared Jess down until Jess turned and walked out.

In the car she checked in with the detachment, told Sturgis what she had found.

"I'll take care of a warrant," Sturgis said. "For her home too. She probably has a computer there. Morell, why don't you go farther afield. Take her picture to Charlotte Ridge and Hawksnest Landing and see if anyone can place her there."

"Right, sir. On my way."

Hawksnest Landing was a tiny community, almost just a crossroads with a small collection of houses and a gas station. There was a boat launch and parking lot next to the river. She pulled into the gas station where an old man, his eyes closed, rocked in a chair outside the door. With a face full of wrinkles that were more like crevasses and white whiskers; he looked close to a hundred years old. Jess made sure she could see him breathing before she left him and went inside. She presented Aimée's picture to Anne, the clerk.

"Sure, I think that's Dr. Chandler, right?" she said.

"Sure, I've been to her. What's happening?" She rubbed her skinny arms as if cold.

"She's missing," Jess said. "You haven't seen her or heard anything about her, have you? She's been missing a few days now."

"Oh, wow. I hope she's alright. She's nice and a good doctor. Looked after my daughter real good." The clerk blew long wispy hair out of her eyes as she talked.

"If you hear anything especially about her movements please give us a call." Jess passed her a business card.

"Sure, Officer. I really hope you find her."

Down the road a few more miles Jess came to the outskirts of Charlotte Ridge. It was much larger than Hawksnest Landing but the town sign said the population was only nine hundred people. She passed some rental cabins and came to the Nilsson General Store where she stopped. The large store bustled with activity. A coffee group sat around an old wooden table in the back corner of the store. Jess eyed the clerk and approached with the picture.

"Hi, I'm Constable Morell."

"Flo Nilsson." Flo reached her hand to Jess's and they shook. "Can I help you with something?"

"I hope so. We're looking for this woman, Dr. Aimée-Marie Chandler. Have you seen her or know of her whereabouts?"

Flo examined the photo. She was a large woman, soft and round in the middle. Short grey hair topped an open friendly face.

"I know who the doctor is but I haven't seen her

around here." She hollered to the coffee group. "Hey, you guys, has anybody seen Dr. Aimée Chandler lately, and I don't mean for your piles, Auggie, I mean, just seen her around?"

Shaking heads. "Nope, not me," Auggie Rymes said.

Jess walked back to the group. "This is her," she said offering the photo." More head shaking.

"I know who she is," said Michael Heath, "but haven't seen her." Heath was dressed in a casual style but sported a cleaner shave than the rest of the group.

"Okay. If you hear anything about her, let Flo know, okay? Or call the detachment."

She thanked Flo and wandered over to the garage. Keith Rymes stopped his work on a white SUV and looked at the picture. Jess remembered his name. He was the drunk in the ER that threatened Dr. Chandler. Jess wondered if he remembered. "We're looking for this woman driving a black 2013 Chevrolet Equinox. Anyone of this description come in here?"

"Naw, sorry. Just this van for now."

"I've seen a report that said you had an altercation with this doctor in the ER one time. Are you a person to hold grudges, Mr. Rymes?"

"What! Grudges? Don't remember nothin' about that fracas, you know, when I was drunk. Don't remember much when I'm drunk, right?"

"You went to jail for a night."

Keith Rymes shrugged.

"And you haven't seen this lady recently?"

"I'd remember that, I would. She's a looker, ain't

she?" He stared at Jess a minute. "You too. What's a good lookin' girl like you doin' in a cop suit?" Jess couldn't miss the sly leer.

"Keep in mind that I carry a gun, fella." Maybe he was good for an assault on Aimée-Marie. He certainly had the bent personality for it.

"Sure, sure," his hands in a defensive gesture. "No harm, no foul."

Jess left Rymes, shaking her hands in the air as if to cleanse them of dirt, and reclaimed the squad car. She was opening the car door when Flo appeared in the doorway of the store.

Flo waved at her to wait. "Hey, Officer, do you know about the commune up on the ridge?"

"Not really, no."

"They're a weird bunch, you know, with Bible robes and beards. You know, like a cult. Strict rules and lots of religious talk. We get all our eggs from them. They have a small egg production business. You should check them out. Take Ridge Road just at the edge of town." She pointed in the direction Jess had come. "Just keep going and you'll run into their commune."

Jess thought that weird people were always worth checking out, if not for now, at least to know what was happening in the area. Keeping with protocol, Jess radioed her new destination to telecoms.

She took the Ridge Road, gravel and wide enough for cars to pass. Just keep going, Flo said. It was a couple of miles in when Jess saw a shelter, probably used by hunters, nestled in the bright green trees, the spring growth like elegant emerald arms lifting to the sky. Jess thought spring months were the most wonderful. There was a small bridge over a creek and then a sign, black paint on weathered plywood nailed to a tree announcing the commune.

Look to God's Glory and Sin No More

Wouldn't it be nice if a sign did it for all the sinners she dealt with, Jess thought. She pulled into the yard and parked beside the nearest house where smoke drifted from a chimney. There were several small structures in the immediate area in good or poor shape looking as if someone had needed shelter in a hurry. All had smoke curling from a chimney. There was one large, long building that must house the laying hens. The house in front of her was in desperate need of a makeover, worn out on all fronts. It had to be an old settler's house from many decades ago, peeling paint, cardboard in the windows, curled shingles and a rotted porch that sagged under foot. Jess knocked on the door.

Hearing the noise, a small girl about five-years-old came around the corner of the house, curiosity on her face. She stopped in her tracks when she saw a stranger in a police uniform. Dressed in a dirty red sweater with a snowflake design, delicate wrists extended from too-short sleeves. She wore a long print dress and rubber boots and carried a woman's purse from which a doll's head protruded.

As they looked at each other, a woman, thirtyish,

thin with tired eyes opened the door, her clothes an ankle-length gray dress and wool socks with sandals. Her face was bruised with a scrape and the woman tried to cover it with her hand. Jess's thoughts immediately went to abuse. "May peace be with you. Can I help you?" she said around her hand. She noticed the child and shooed her away. "Verity, this is no concern of yours," she told her. The child scampered away.

"Perhaps you can help me," Jess said.

"With God's help," the woman said.

"Sister! I'll answer the door." A tall, lanky man appeared in the room coming from a back door, a bundle of firewood in his arms. He dropped it beside the wood stove. He wore a long beige robe and heavy work boots. His brown hair and beard almost reached the leather belt cinching his waist. The woman meekly stepped back to the kitchen area. "Neither is this your concern, Sister Judith," he said more gently to the woman. He was easy to read, either the type of man who intimidated a woman or hardened her resolve. Jess found the steel in her spine.

"Who am I speaking to?" she asked with authority in her voice and hand resting on her service weapon, a nine millimeter Smith and Wesson.

"Brother Jedidiah. What can I do for you?"

"Constable Morell. We are scouring the area looking for this woman," she said holding out the picture. "She's been missing for several days,"

He barely gave it a look. "We keep to ourselves

and don't see many people." His eyes shifted back to Jess's face.

"She's a doctor by the name of Aimée-Marie Chandler. If you hear anything or see anything that could lead us to her, please give a call to this number." She handed him a card. She looked over at Sister Judith in the kitchen. "Or if we can help in any way," she said pointedly.

"As I said, we don't mix." Now he was closing the door. Jess stuck her foot out to block it, as much to establish her authority as relay a message.

"If you would let the other people who live here know about her."

"Thank you, Constable. Good day." The door closed.

Weird bunch indeed.

As Jess walked away from the porch the little girl came around the corner again. This time the purse was slung across her chest and the naked doll in her arms. A young woman was holding her hand. She was dressed in the simple style and looked about seventeen or eighteen years old, fresh-faced and with eyes that still had spirit. In another setting she would fit right in with high school cheer leaders. Jess walked over to her.

"Hi, I'm Officer Morell. Jessica. And you are…?"

A hesitation. "Charity."

"Charity. That's a pretty name. I've never been here before. Do you like it here, Charity?"

The girl's lips parted to reply, then, a shrug.

"Having met Brother Jedidiah and looking around

here I think this could be a difficult way to live," She waited for reaction. "Charity, if you ever need help, if you are scared about anything that is happening, find a phone, call nine-one-one. Got that. Nine-one-one." The girls stared at Jess. Verity turned her face up to the older girl as if seeking reassurance. Charity ran a hand gently over Verity's hair, then, gestured with a head bob that she got the message. Jess left them standing in the yard, following her with their eyes as she started the car.

As she pulled away, she heard a phone ring. The young child startled. Jess saw Charity quickly hustle Verity away from the house and they disappeared from view. Probably a contraband phone, Jess thought.

You wouldn't find her living here, not for a million dollars.

CHAPTER 5

AɪᴍÉᴇ'ꜱ ᴘᴀʀᴇɴᴛꜱ, Kᴇʟʟʏ ᴀɴᴅ Mᴇᴇɴᴀ Carlisle, just arrived from Ontario, sat at the dining table in their daughter's house. Adam poured coffee.

"Maybe you'd like something stronger. It's gotta be cocktail time somewhere."

"Oh, Adam, I wouldn't mind, actually," his mother-in-law said, eyes red from weeping. "Kelly? Coffee or other?"

Kelly, medium build and greying with a bald patch, leaned his elbows onto the table. "Coffee followed by other," he said grimly. "But, I don't think there's enough whiskey in the country to numb me sufficiently. Adam, are you sure this small town police force is doing all they should? I mean, what resources do they have?"

"I hate to say it, and as angry as I've been that this is taking so long, but, they have access to everything a bigger detachment would have. The RCMP tech and manpower support is there. Her picture and the details are out to the media and the public so I just don't know what to do next."

"You don't know if she might have gone somewhere, had a breakdown or something?" Meena asked. Adam handed her a drink which she poured into her coffee. Aimée was a clone of her mother, slim with chestnut hair. She had delicate features and a face that revealed every emotion she felt. Adam felt Aimée's presence as he looked at his mother-in-law.

"I don't know anything." He ran a hand over his hair. "The thing is… her travel bag is missing. She keeps one partially packed with things she doesn't want to forget like a small toothbrush, slippers, hair care products, that kind of thing. It must be in her car, but I don't know why."

"She didn't have any plans to go away, one of her retreats?" Kelly Carlisle, hope in his voice, had downed half his whiskey in one gulp.

"None that she mentioned. We've called everyone we know, retreats, friends, colleagues. No one can tell us anything."

"So what do we do now? Just sit here and drink, hope that she'll walk in the door? It's unbelievable." The whiskey hadn't settled Kelly, seemed to agitate him. No longer seated, he paced the kitchen, his face wrinkled in worry.

"I guess you've contacted Derrick," Adam said.

"Yeah, we phoned. He wants to come home but we told him to wait a bit. Maybe this will soon turn out for the better." Aimée-Marie's brother was an engineer working at a job in Thailand.

Meena Carlisle, trim and well-groomed in navy sweater and pants broke down in tears, again. "I can't believe this is happening. I wish someone would help us." She sobbed as Kelly stopped his pacing and pulled her close.

"Come, Meena. Maybe you should lie down for a while. Have a rest," Kelly said softly. She nodded.

"Here, I'll take your things to your room. You know which one. I'm afraid I didn't make the bed but I'll get the linens." Adam took the bags from the entrance hall and deposited them in the guest room. He got clean bedding and placed it on the bed. Kelly and Meena followed him. The room was comfortably furnished in a modern style, soft grey walls with a teal carpet. A large window let in soft early evening sunlight.

"I'll help Meena make the bed. Thanks, Adam."

"Towels in the bathroom when you want to freshen up."

Kelly settled Meena covering her with one of the colourful quilts she had made and gifted to Aimée and Adam. She closed her eyes and her breathing evened into an easy rhythm.

Kelly joined Adam in the living room. Adam refreshed their drinks.

"This whole thing has been devastating," Adam said. "I haven't worked since the day she went missing. I can't. I'm far too distracted."

"What's happening to your practice?"

"Several colleagues are dividing up the calls."

"I can't help but say you look like hell."

"Doesn't surprise me a bit. I haven't been paying much attention." He breathed deeply, a cleansing breath. The landline in the kitchen rang and Adam jumped to answer it. "Maybe something," he said over his shoulder.

"What?" Kelly heard Adam say. "What are you saying? Don't do this!" He hung up. Hearing that Adam was upset, Kelly had come into the kitchen.

"What was that? Some news?"

Adam sank into a chair a hand covering his mouth, shock on his face. "Someone said 'I know you killed her. You'll be punished for your sin.'"

"What?" Disbelief.

"Someone thinks I killed her. He actually said that." Adam looked beseechingly at Kelly. "How could someone do that?"

"That's… that's disgusting. Did you recognize the voice?"

"No."

Kelly checked the caller ID. "Unknown Caller." They both sat there for a moment, stunned. "Come back into the living room. I'll screen calls from now on," Kelly said.

"No. You don't have to listen to that."

"Neither do you." After a thoughtful moment, "Should you call the cops, let them know?"

"I can't take anymore right now. I'll call them in the morning."

They sat solemnly with their drinks and their misery willing the best possible outcome.

❧❧

Jess returned to the detachment just before shift change. She told Sturgis what she had learned for her time, which amounted to the information that Aimée met a man after yoga on two occasions. It wasn't much, but, the word was out there about a missing woman. She told Sturgis about Keith Rymes and the religious commune.

"Good to know," he said. "Tolerance may be in short supply there so we'll keep them all on our radar."

She found Todd staring at her from across the room as if he wanted to say something. She was writing up her notes when he approached the desk.

"How about a bite to eat, Jess? We could go easy at a fast food place or have a more relaxed dinner somewhere else."

"I… oh, Todd I'm really looking forward to a night in with a grilled cheese. I'm tired. Another time?"

"Oh, sure, if that's what you want. Maybe another day." He didn't look happy. It seemed to mean a lot to him.

She reconsidered. "Okay. Maybe a quick burger at McDonald's." Todd smiled broadly. She returned to her work. She didn't want to encourage Todd. He was nice but, there wasn't any magic there. She was looking for more. Any girl would.

At shift change, Jess and Todd, each driving their own car, met at the nearby McDonald's. The odour of greasy grilled beef filled the place. Sometimes Jess welcomed it and sometimes she didn't. Tonight she didn't. It would be chicken on a bun with a Diet Coke to wash it down. Todd dug into a Quarter Pounder and fries.

"So, what are your thoughts on the missing Dr. Chandler?" Todd wiped grease from his mouth with a napkin.

Jess was thoughtful not wanting to expose any naiveté in her answer. "I'm inclined to believe Dr. Adam for the moment. She may have taken off with a lover but that's a pretty strange thing to do in the middle of the night after a hospital call. You'd think that would take more planning But, her car's missing, her travel bag is gone. If it had been a weekend, well, I just don't know. There are too many possibilities. What do you think?"

Todd looked around and kept his voice low. "You don't think he did away with her?"

Jess, not thinking that scenario worked for her said, "Well, as I said, anything is possible."

"Yeah, possible. She could have come home and they had a rip-roaring fight and he killed her. When you love someone and she betrays you… he could have known about a lover."

"The neighbours say there has never been a problem there, no loud fights, nothing to suggest they weren't getting along."

"But if your wife or girlfriend gets it on with someone else, it's pretty easy to whip up anger." He put down his burger and his hands tightened into fists as he leaned across at Jess.

"Enough to kill?" Jess looked back at him quizzically. He looked like he could whip into anger at the thought of betrayal.

"I think I understand crimes of passion, that's all I'm saying." His hands relaxed and he resumed eating.

It was a revealing answer. Whatever you do don't get into a love triangle with Todd, Jess thought. Like that was likely to happen. She scoffed at the notion.

Meal finished they parted at their cars. "There's a nice hot bath waiting for me followed by reading in bed," Jess said. "Are you on shift tomorrow?"

"Yeah, eight to six."

"Me too. See you then." Jess didn't notice that Todd was slow to get into his car and watched as Jess pulled out of the parking lot.

Jess's apartment building was in an area that was older and well-treed with small family homes on each side of the street. The sun was low in the sky but the April night hadn't yet fallen and Jess enjoyed the warm feel of her neighbourhood. She wondered how a multi-unit building ended up on this block but figured someone in authority had turned a blind eye to zoning. She didn't mind. The surroundings were nice on the outside if not spacious on the inside.

Soon she was immersed in her bath, the heat easing tired muscles. She felt loose and languid as she dried herself off. Donning pajamas and a robe she wandered to the bedroom window while rubbing a towel over her wet hair.

She peered into the darkening street. Was that a person who just pulled back behind that clump of trees trying to hide himself? A tall figure? She leaned into the window and cupped her hand around her eyes for a better view. Certainly nothing there now. If it was a person, what was he doing? What were his intentions? She squinted and decided she must be seeing shadows of the trees. There was a bit of a wind. The trees were moving, not a person.

She thought back a few weeks. She'd seen shadows then, too, hadn't she? Same place, almost the same time. In the morning she would take a look at that clump of trees and see if there was anything tangible at the site to support the idea of a prowler.

She climbed into bed and picked up her book dismissing the shadows as the Michael Connelly mystery in her hands unfolded. But, before settling for the night she got up and looked out the window again. Nothing moved. The shadows were still. She went back to bed feeling reassured.

CHAPTER 6

BEFORE WORK, JESS CROSSED THE street to inspect the stand of bushes and trees in the empty lot which faced her apartment. She tried to gauge the area visible from her bedroom window. Circling the bushes she stood looking at her apartment and found the most likely spot. She noted disturbance in the soft dirt and a few broken twigs and crushed leaves and knew her sightings weren't shadows. There had been a person standing here last night and probably the time before that when the night shadows were moving.

It was spooky. Was she the target? Was someone lurking about trying to catch a glimpse of her in her bedroom? It made her shudder. She looked to the neighbours' houses and decided to do a quick survey. Knocking at doors she found people still in housecoats or fresh out of the shower.

"There are indications that someone is prowling the area. Did you see anything suspicious last night?"

She was met with denial on both sides of the empty lot and across the street.

"Do we have anything to worry about?" they asked, concern on their faces.

"Just be vigilant and lock your doors and windows. Call nine-one-one if you see anything suspicious." Jess left business cards and drove on to work.

After checking in she told Sturgis about the incident. He said he'd arrange a frequent drive-pass of her place for the coming nights.

Jess sat at her desk. Today, she would take any calls about Aimée-Marie Chandler. Since the public appeal the phone had been active. All information was checked out but most was a waste of time. And then there was call from Kelowna. The caller identified herself as Stephanie McCleery.

"She was seeing my husband," the woman on the phone told Jess.

"What do you mean seeing?" Jess asked to clarify.

"Well, he's a doctor but I don't mean he was seeing her for medical reasons. Although, he certainly examined her anatomy, if you know what I mean." The woman's tone crackled with bitterness.

"You're telling me he was having an affair with Aimée-Marie Chandler?" Jess sat up straighter.

"Yes! That's exactly what I'm telling you! I saw her picture on TV and if she's missing he might have something to do with it."

"What makes you say that? Have you known him to be violent?" Jess scribbled notes as she spoke.

"Oh, he can be violent. His patients think he's God's gift but I know better. More like the devil's gift. I've had the bruises to prove it."

"How do you know he's been seeing her?"

"I saw them together, didn't I? I followed him one time. He told me he had a meeting. It was during a medical conference here in Kelowna. He had a meeting, alright, in her hotel room."

"So you were suspicious because…"

"He's been unfaithful before, hasn't he?" The words spit from her mouth.

"You don't think it was a meeting of colleagues for business reasons?"

"He'd showered before he came home! I could tell! No, the only business happening was funny business."

"And when did this happen? Do you know dates?"

"Of course. It was during the conference which was the middle of January. You can check her hotel reservation."

"And how can I best reach your husband?"

"Probably his office." She gave Jess the phone number of the office and of his cell phone. "Don't know where he's living. Just know it isn't here anymore."

"Thank you, Mrs. McCleery. We may have to talk to you again."

"Won't be Mrs. McCleery for long. Can't wait to get rid of that snake's name." The phone call stopped abruptly as Stephanie McCleery ended the connection. In Jess's opinion she was a bitter, angry woman and the information had to be filtered through that lens. Maybe everything she said was true, maybe embellished by wishing it to be true.

She found Sturgis and related the call.

"She could be just trying to cause trouble for her husband. Wouldn't be the first time in a divorce." He thought for a moment. "Call his office. What's his name?"

"Hugh McCleery."

"Set up a skype interview with Dr. McCleery. If we think we need to see him in person we'll take it from there. We might just have the first solid motive for Dr. Chandler as the perp."

Or for a scorned lover capable of violence, Jess thought. It could go either way.

Meena Carlisle had had a bad night. The emotions of the last several days had taken a toll. Her face was carved with deep lines that Adam had never seen before. Red-rimmed eyes told Adam that the weeping continued. Kelly was less solicitous of his wife today. Adam could tell he was trying to bolster her for what might come. They could possibly be in the spotlight as time went on.

"Come, Meena. Eat for strength if not for enjoyment." He spooned scrambled eggs onto the plate in front of her and added toast as Adam buttered it.

"Meena," Adam said, "tonight I think you should take a sedative so you can sleep. Maybe even take a mild one now to take the edge off your distress."

"Tonight, okay. But not now. I want to be totally

in the moment when Aimée comes back." She took a small bite of toast.

Adam and Kelly looked at each other neither knowing how to respond.

"Okay, tonight, then," Adam said. He sat with the food in front of him and tried to eat. He knew how Meena felt; he just couldn't give in to it.

The kitchen fell into quiet, Adam pouring more coffee for everyone, Meena finally settling into a slow recovery from the weepy spell.

"I'll call the police station later and see if anything has changed overnight," Adam said. He made a phoning gesture which told Kelly he was going to report the accusing phone call from last night. Kelly nodded. Neither thought it was a good idea to tell Meena.

Then, from outside came scratching, shuffling sounds of someone at the door. When the bell didn't ring, Adam got up to see what was happening. He opened the door just as two people, young men in hoodies, ran from the doorway, across the front lawn and into a waiting truck. They sped away with a screech of tires peeling rubber as they went. Beside Adam on the door front in dripping red paint was the word KILLER.

Adam's face reddened and veins in his neck bulged as fury grew. "God damn them! God damn them!" he spit. Kelly was beside him, silent in absorbing what had happened.

"God damn them is right!" Kelly finally said. "How can they think you'd hurt Aimée? How can anyone?" They both stood there staring at the damage. Adam, clearly, was paralyzed. Finally, Kelly took charge. "You call the police. I'm going to take a picture of this then wash it off. It's still wet. It may not clean off perfectly but nobody will be able to read it."

Adam stood there, pain in his eyes, the anger dissipated, replaced by despair. "This is a nightmare," he said with emotion. "I want to wake up."

"So do we all," Kelly said. He put his arm across Adam's shoulders and led him inside.

The skype interview was scheduled for one p.m. Sturgis said he would take the lead. Sturgis along with Jess and Todd Henley gathered in an interview room and logged on.

"Dr. McCleery, I'm Staff Sergeant Sturgis with the Cranbrook RCMP. Thank you for talking with us. In the room with me are Constable Morell and Constable Henley."

"I don't know how I can help you but I'll try. I've never had any business in Cranbrook." McCleery sat behind his desk. Jess could see framed diplomas on the wall behind him. He had that distinguished look that professionals cultivate with groomed hair and expensive suits. Jess thought his tie, alone, had to cost one hundred dollars. He still had a winter suntan either from skiing or a vacation somewhere warm. Jess thought he gave off a narcissistic vibe. Perhaps it was just talking to his wife made it feel that way.

"Sir," Sturgis said, "we believe you know a woman

from Cranbrook who has gone missing. We're talking to as many of her associates as we can. It's Aimée-Marie Chandler. Can you tell us how you know her?"

"Ah, yes, Dr. Chandler. I saw that on the news. So distressing." Jess thought he was stalling to organize his response. "Dr. Chandler came to a medical conference in Kelowna last January. Many of us met her. We're all colleagues, so to speak." He smoothed his shirt-front with a manicured hand.

"When was the last time you saw her, doctor?"

"Why, at the conference, of course."

"Doctor," Sturgis's tone hardened. "We have a witness that tells us your relationship with Dr. Chandler was more than just as colleagues. That it was personal. We need to know if you have seen her or heard from her since January."

"Personal! That's an outrageous statement. A witness, you say. Someone is being malicious and I can guess who. My wife is behind this, isn't she?"

"Doctor, this is a very serious matter. If you have heard from Dr. Chandler we need to know. Her husband is very distraught. There has to be an explanation for her disappearance."

"I know nothing about her disappearance. Yes, I have talked to her. We confer sometimes. She has a brilliant mind."

"So it's her mind you're interested in?"

"Look, I don't need your insinuations. I've talked to you willingly and you practically accuse me of an affair. It's not on, Sergeant."

"You brought up the word affair, Doctor." The doctor's face visibly blanched. "It would explain a lot if she had plans to meet you somewhere and never showed up. There are many ways this could play out. If your relationship with Dr. Chandler is personal it can mean a change in the direction of our investigation."

McCleery was silent, debating his next move, debating what to tell them. He pulled on his tie then patted it down. "Okay, look, I like Aimée-Marie. We had a good time at the conference. She might have taken more from my attention than I meant to convey. She's called me a lot, wanting to see me, wanting more than the one hook-up we had. So I met her once about two months ago. She keeps calling me. The last I heard from her was two weeks ago. It was more of the same."

"The same meaning..."

"She wanted to get together, to... deepen, if you will, our relationship. I put her off as best I could."

"Did she say anything about going away?"

"On her own or with me?"

"Either, we're just trying to find her."

"She was almost frantic about coming to see me. I discouraged it. Strongly. She's a clinging person, much too clinging for my taste."

"Did that make you angry, sir?"

"Angry?" Silence for a minute. "Yeah, sort of. I had to speak strongly to her, tell her there was nothing more between us. She didn't like it and went away spitting some angry words. She was volatile. I don't need that."

"Did she ever become physically abusive with you? I mean striking out?"

"During our two times together? No. She came on strong, though, with… sex, if I can say that, but, not abusive. But it was close to the surface. I think she could fly off pretty easily." McCleery looked at his watch. "I have to go. I have office hours. I've been as helpful as I know how to be. You will be discrete about this, Sergeant, won't you?"

"If at all possible, yes. Thank you, Dr. McCleery. We appreciate your time. Perhaps we'll have to talk again."

They signed off.

"So," Sturgis said, "what do you think?'

Jess and Todd looked at each other. Jess replied, "He gave himself a motive whether he realized it or not. A lover coming on too strong, wife at home looking for ways to nail him in a divorce. He might have decided to permanently rid her from his life."

"He's self-confident enough to think he could get away with saying what he did," Sturgis observed. "We need a background on Dr. McCleery. Todd that's for you. I want to know if there is anything in his credit card or phone records that suggest they met more than twice like he said."

"Yes, sir. But, maybe Dr. Adam found out about it and took matters into his own hands," Todd said.

"We're back at the husband, then," Sturgis said. "And the search warrants aren't going to work. The judge said there wasn't probable cause to search the home or office. He said Aimée-Marie is an adult and can leave home if she wants to. We have no evidence that implicates the husband or that a crime has even been committed so, we have to get the husband's consent. We need to examine the house for forensics and her computer to see if she used it to talk to anybody, make any plans."

Sturgis's phone chirped. He was brief. "Colleen says Dr. Adam is on the line. Something about trouble at his house. Jess, you're with me. We're going out there to see what's up." In a curt reply to Dr. Adam he said that they were on the way.

Kelly Carlisle was cleaning the door as they arrived. Adam came to his side as Jess and Sturgis walked up to the house. "What happened here?" Sturgis said. Kelly showed him the picture of the defaced door.

Adam, who had swung between anger and despair, erupted into anger at Sturgis. "Look what this has come to! Look! People think I'm a killer! You have to stop this!"

"We haven't done anything to provoke it," Sturgis said evenly.

"Like hell you haven't! There must be a leak in your department! Somehow the public knows what's on your mind. You suspect me don't you? I can tell. Obviously the public can to." Kelly put a hand on Adam's arm, said some calming words. Adam pulled away. "I'm being treated like a criminal. Plug your leak, Sergeant." He turned away into the house. The loud voices had brought Meena to the door.

"Kelly?" she said, worry and curiosity coming together.

Kelly sheltered her with his arm and turned her indoors.

"May we come in, Dr. Chandler? I want to discuss something with you." Not hearing a refusal, Sturgis and Jess entered the foyer. "Dr. Chandler, we need to look deeper into your wife's life. We need access to her home computer to see if there is anything on it that would be a clue to her whereabouts."

Adam wiped hands over his face, tired and wrung out and replied quietly. "Don't you think I've already done that?"

"Well, sir, our tech department has ways of finding things that maybe you can't. If you would let us take it to the detachment... things that have been deleted, can be retrieved..."

"I can't do that," Adam said. "She has patient information on it. I've already looked for anything related to this. I know how to look in the recycle bin! It's not there!"

"It's more than that. Our techs can dig deeper. And maybe the patient information is important to her whereabouts. Maybe someone threatened her. We can have a doctor or lawyer standing beside the tech to screen for sensitive material coming up."

"Get a warrant for her office computer."

"Sir, we want to do everything we can to find her. This is important," he said in an imploring tone.

"So is patient confidentiality. The answer is no. I've

looked! If I find anything that seems suspicious I'll let you know." His face was tight with sharp lines.

"Adam," Kelly said, "don't you think you could let them, just this once."

"No, Kelly. You don't understand. I just can't."

"Dr. Chandler, could we send a team in to go over your house. Sometimes there are clues that you don't see but experts do."

Adam's head shot up. "And then what? The world sees me even more as a suspect and I get more vandalism. I had a phone call last night, anonymous, calling me a murderer! This has to stop! There's nothing here, Sergeant, nothing to help. I've looked. Believe me, I've looked." He stood and turned his back on the officers as he started to leave the room. "Look in her office computer, but not here. Now, please, leave."

Chandler's back was up but this wasn't the time to mention his wife's infidelity in front of her parents. It would keep until tomorrow. "We can put a trace on your phone, a digital number recorder. Nothing has to be anonymous. Will you let us do that?"

"Yes," Adam said quietly. He sounded as if he'd caved in. "Come and do that."

"Yes, sir. I'll send a tech."

They left. In the car Sturgis turned to Jess. "It doesn't look good that he wouldn't allow access to the house and computer." He was thoughtful a moment, drummed his fingers on the steering wheel. Finally he said, "You found that Aimée's life insurance policy was $200,000?"

"Yeah, that's what they said."

"That's a lot of motive," he said and started the engine. "And why won't he let forensics examine the house? Maybe because there's blood splatter on the floor and walls." Jess looked at the firm set of Sturgis' jaw and knew that Adam Chandler was even more in the crosshairs.

Inside, Kelly and Meena watched Adam's retreating back with confusion. Both thought Adam should be cooperating with the police in every possible way. They wanted their daughter back at any cost. Adam should too. They looked at each other in bewilderment.

"Shouldn't he have done more?" Meena asked.

"Yeah, that's what I thought."

That evening, Jess went over all that had happened that day. The prowler, McCleery's admission of a sexual relationship with Aimée-Marie, the vandalism and Dr. Adam's refusal to allow an inspection of his house and home computer, the large sum that was life insurance.

Did that add up to Dr. Adam as a killer? What happened inside that house? Where is Aimée-Marie Chandler? Were they getting closer to the truth?

She didn't like the idea that Dr. Adam was withholding information. She'd rather think of him as a victim. He was too soft, too distraught, too…, actually he had an appealing vulnerability, the kind of thing that melts a woman's heart. But, she didn't really know him, and neither did Sturgis. The staff sergeant was just reacting as an experienced policeman. She was reacting — okay, she'd admit it in the seclusion of her bedroom — as a woman. Adam Chandler had stirred things in her that were unprofessional. She had to stop that. He could be as guilty as sin.

She stood by her window, the shadows of the night sky deepening to black. She unwrapped her wet hair from the towel and brushed it with long even strokes. It was a soothing ritual, a prelude to sleep.

The shadows moved. As had happened last night, there was movement in that clump of trees. She peered through the window, face cupped by hands touching the glass and couldn't make out details. She threw the brush onto the bed, jumped into jeans and a sweatshirt, and strapped her utility belt around her waist. She dashed down the stairs and out the door running across the street to confront whoever was lurking there.

She ran until she reached the curb then, with stealth, circled the clump of trees. She pulled the flashlight from her belt. Standing there in the circle of light, phone to his ear, was Todd Henley.

"What? Todd? What in the hell are you doing here?" Anger flared and subsided. The details weren't computing. Why would Todd be standing behind the trees?

"Oh, Jess. Everything's okay. I was just phoning you," He indicated the phone. "I heard what you told Sturgis and thought I'd look around as well as the patrol cars. Has there been anything this evening? I wanted to ask," he said with the phone aloft.

"Nothing but you, Todd. Why would you scare the wits out of me like this? From my window you look like the prowler. I came here ready to arrest someone." Her heart was still tripping.

"I haven't seen anyone. I sat in my car down the street for a while. No action at all."

"Well, I'm glad to hear that. But your car might have scared off the prowler, for tonight at least. Did you think of that?"

"Right, right. But at least you're safe. That's what matters, Jess, that you're safe." His voice softened to a caress.

"Um, yeah, I guess, thanks. I guess we can call it a night." She turned to go.

"Uh, Jess, there wouldn't be a cup of tea going, would there?" It was almost a plea.

Had Todd gone out of his way to protect her? Was he just a bystander? What had he been doing on her street in front of her building that day? Could he possibly be a stalker? Did she owe him at least a cup of tea for looking out for her or...

"Sure, I guess. It'll help settle nerves all around. C'mon, what kind do you like?"

CHAPTER 7

Meena and Kelly Carlisle drank coffee and ate breakfast without Adam. The police had called Adam to the detachment again. As the days passed, their distress didn't diminish but rather increased as the sinking realization that their daughter might never return settled deeper into their minds. Meena still had weepy spells but the offer of a sedative from Adam helped in the night time hours. This morning she had managed to eat oatmeal and toast and Kelly squeezed her hand telling her, "Good job."

They sat in silence each absorbed by their own thoughts. At one point each looked at the other and held the gaze.

"I think you're thinking about it too," Kelly said.

"It?" Meena feigned ignorance.

"You know what I mean," Kelly said clutching a coffee mug. "You know you can't get that word killer out of your mind."

Meena sighed deeply. "No, I can't. It cuts so deep, it's so ugly. Even with the sedative last night I had nightmares. I actually dreamed that Adam turned his back on Aimée, walked away from her when she was calling him for help."

"If it were only that simple." A thoughtful pause, then, he said quietly, "Maybe she did call for help." He turned haunted eyes to his wife.

"Kelly! What are you suggesting?"

Kelly hesitated not wanting to say it out loud. It would make the possibility real if he said it out loud. "You know…"

"No! No! Adam has always been a loving husband. You know how affectionate he is. He would never do anything to harm Aimée."

"I know, I know. It's a horrible thought. But, why wouldn't he cooperate with the police yesterday? Maybe it's not so much what Aimée has on the computer but what he has. Maybe *he* doesn't want them digging deep into the marriage. What is he hiding?"

Each settled back into coffee and their thoughts when several whacks against the house roused them to look outside. They peered around the edge of the door in time to see four young men throwing eggs which landed with a splat against the cedar siding.

Kelly was out the door in a split second shouting at them. "You bastards! Take off! I'm calling the police!"

One final egg was thrown as the group laughed and shouted back. "He deserves worse, the murderer!

Murderer!" They hurled the words before taking off at a gallop reveling in their work.

The siding was a mess. Kelly took a picture then started hosing it before the egg dried in place. This had undone Meena who was crying silently, again. It was apparent that the court of public opinion had found Adam guilty.

Maybe, maybe with Adam gone he could take a look at the computer. That thought took form until he couldn't see not doing it. Adam's lack of cooperation left a huge question mark. Meena would back him up.

"Meena, what if those… vandals know something we don't. We don't live here. We don't know what kind of rumours swirl around town. We don't really know what kind of marriage our daughter has with Adam. Has she ever told you anything?"

"Our conversations are all about her work, house decorating, her yoga class. No, nothing too personal about their marriage."

He waited a thoughtful minute. "I'm going to do it."

"What? Look at the computer?" The worry lines that creased her face slackened into acceptance. "I think it's the right thing to do. For us. For our peace of mind. For Aimée."

Kelly bobbed his head and went to the third bedroom used as an office. Meena hung over Kelly's shoulder as he opened the screen. Emails were password protected but other files weren't. Kelly started scrolling.

"Thank You for coming in, Dr. Chandler." Sturgis was using his polite approach today probably hoping it would induce the doctor to allow a search at his home. Adam Chandler sat opposite Sturgis and Jess in the interview room. He had shaved this morning and clothes were casual and fresh. But, his eyes still had a haunted look.

"Did I have a choice?" Adam said.

"Unless we arrest you you always have a choice."

Adam harrumphed as a reply. "So, are we going over it once again, the same territory to see if I say anything different this time?" He sat back in the chair, resigned to this next round of interrogation.

"Actually, no. We have some information we want to share. But, maybe it isn't news to you that your wife had an affair." He waited for the reaction.

Adam swallowed as his face hardened.

"No comment, doctor? We've spoken with the man, a doctor in Kelowna and he admits to it. The affair was brief but it happened. What can you tell us about that, Doctor? Tell us how you felt when you discovered it. Tell us how much you wanted to hurt your wife for her betrayal. I'm waiting, Doctor." By this time he was leaning across the table peering into Adam's face.

Oh, God, McCleery too. It was a gut-punch that left him momentarily speechless.

Finally he said, "I love my wife. I want to find her. I didn't hurt Aimée. I would never hurt her. If... if she had an affair it's something we would have dealt with. Marriages don't have to fall apart because of one indiscretion." He looked into his lap.

"How very understanding of you Dr. Chandler. Not all husbands would react that way. I know I wouldn't."

"But then, you're a bully and I'm not."

Sturgis jumped across the desk and fisted the front of Adam's shirt. "You'll be respectful during this interview, Doctor."

Jess was beside him pulling back on his arm. "Staff Sergeant Sturgis, easy does it."

Sturgis let go of the shirt and gathered himself with a deep breath. "I know you did something to her and I won't quit until you're behind bars."

"Thank you, Staff Sergeant. You just gave me my walking papers. Any future interview will be with my lawyer present." He stood, adjusted his jacket and walked out of the room.

Adam's heart pounded as he made his way to his car. He'd finally had enough. He wouldn't start defending his marriage to a person like Sturgis — especially with it so hard to defend. To hell with Sturgis and the whole police detachment. It was time to assert his rights.

His anger and hurt simmered on the way home. So McCleery wasn't just a colleague but a lover. His investigative source hadn't said that. Approaching the front door he could see recent cleaning attempts that lacked completion. The window and cedar siding were smeared with gluey egg residue. That stoked the anger further and he yanked on the door handle like it was responsible for the mess.

"What the hell happened?" he yelled to the quiet

house. "Did those felons throw eggs again?" There was no response.

Kelly and Meena appeared in the doorway of the upstairs bedroom. Their faces registered shock and a fleeting embarrassment at being caught in a room that wasn't common space.

"Who are Hugh McCleery and Kevin Aikens?" Kelly asked accusingly. "You were having Aimée followed, weren't you?"

"Kelly, I…,"

"What? Treated my daughter like a criminal? Spied on her activities? What, Adam? What are you keeping from the police?"

"Come down and sit in the living room, Kelly, Meena." He gestured for them to come down.

They looked at each other and could see no alternative. "We need to hear what he has to say," Kelly told Meena. They slowly descended the stairs.

Once seated on the sofa with Adam in a chair across from them Adam said quietly, "You decided to invade my privacy by scrolling through the computer. You thought you had some kind of right because she's your daughter."

Kelly and Meena looked into their laps then Kelly said defiantly, "You wouldn't cooperate with the police. She's our daughter, our beloved daughter." He choked over the word beloved. "We had to see what you're hiding."

"And you found it." He waited for questions. None

came. "I know a guy, ex- RCMP. He did a job for me. Surveillance."

"In other words, a job of spying on your wife."

"Well, it told a tale I didn't want to hear. I didn't want to let the police have the information because I really think they have a leak in their station. I didn't want it to become part of the rumour mill." Kelly and Meena sat still, waiting for the blow they knew was coming. "Kevin Aikens and Hugh McCleery are men that Aimée has had affairs with."

The Carlisles gasped, "No!"

"I'm afraid yes. Until today I only knew about Aikens. I thought McCleery was just a colleague. He's doing some interesting work with alcohol abuse… well, anyway," he took a deep breath. "Her behavior has been unpredictable for a couple of years now. She explained everything as stress and needing time away from her practice. I found that hard to believe. Aimée loves her work, seems to thrive on it. Then every once in a while she takes off for a few days, a week, supposedly alone to destress and recoup. I got suspicious and hired the ex- cop to find out what was going on."

"If this is true, you realize you just gave yourself a good motive to harm Aimée."

"Another reason I didn't want the police knowing. But they do now. I'm just back from being accused of killing my wife and threatened with prison. They know about Hugh McCleery. They didn't mention Kevin Aikens."

"And you have no idea where Aimée is?" Meena said in a tiny voice.

"Are you accusing me too?" Meena looked embarrassed at his question.

"Is there anything else we don't know?" Emboldened, Kelly asked, "Have you had affairs too?"

Adam's face tightened into a furious mask. "No! Never! I love Aimée. I want our marriage to work. I confronted her about Aikens–he's the one I knew about– and she said it was over, please believe that it wouldn't happen again, etc. She was tearful and contrite. We were trying to piece things together. I thought we were making progress. Then this happened."

"And now you know there's a second man. Are there any more?" Kelly said slowly absorbing the facts.

Adam shrugged. "That's a big question, isn't it?"

"Don't you realize that one of those men could have done something to her, that the police should know?" Kelly went on, "or someone else," he finished meekly.

"I held back what I knew, I know, maybe stupid." A pause as the Carlisles stared at him. "Okay, definitely stupid. I didn't want the whole town to know. I needed it to be private. But they know now about McCleery and they aren't thinking in terms of the man harming her but me doing it if I found out about the affair." Adam scrubbed his face. "I've been overwhelmed and feel like I'm treading water, just holding it together, and sometimes not too successfully."

"This is such a mess," Kelly said. "A shock and a mess." Meena was crying again. Kelly's frustration surfaced. "Oh, for Christ's sake." He left her to it and went outside to calm himself.

"Adam," Meena said through her tears, "You should have told us. Maybe we could have talked to her, helped in some way."

"Aimée didn't want you to know. She made that clear."

"But, Kevin Aikens? Isn't that her friend's husband?"

"Right. Cathy's husband."

"That's… that's so difficult, to say the least."

"Especially since I punched him out when I found out. He promised it was over a year ago. He wanted to stay in his marriage. Cathy didn't know. We decided to keep it that way. Leave them to their mess as long as Aimée wasn't part of it."

The phone chirped and interrupted their talk. Adam recognized his office calling.

"How are things going?" asked his office assistant, Maureen.

"Worse as the days go on," Adam said.

"Well, they're worse here too. Quite a number of patients have asked that their records be sent to a new doctor. Do you think you're coming back anytime soon? I keep putting off patients calling for appointments but can't do it much longer."

"Yeah, okay. Maybe it's time to call in a locum." He was thoughtful and resigned. Maureen jumped in, "Dr. Rhonda Shepherd is finishing up a locum with the clinic. Shall I ask her if she'll come here, should I say indefinitely?"

The word indefinitely startled him but was the reality of the situation. "Yes, I like Rhonda and I think my patients will too. Thanks, Maureen. Set up an appointment with her so I can talk to her about some things."

"Right." She was silent a moment.

"Anything else?"

"Actually, yes. Uh, there have been two threatening phone calls to the office."

"Threatening?"

"Yeah. Like one saying they'll burn down the office if you come back to work. And the second one threatened you personally. He said you weren't fit to be a doctor. I'm sorry, Adam, really sorry."

"Call the police and let them know about the calls. Look out for yourself. I don't think you're in danger but, you never know."

"Maybe I'll just take a few days off until the locum can start. There's no call for any danger once that happens."

"A very good idea. Leave a message on the machine and a sign on the door that the office will open again soon."

"Who's looking after Aimée's patients?" Maureen asked.

"The clinic doctors are sharing them."

"I'm so sorry, Adam."

"So am I." He choked as he closed the phone.

CHAPTER 8

THE WEATHER COOPERATED WITH JESS'S plans to spend her day off canoeing on the St. Mary River. It was her first time on the water this spring and she bubbled with the energizing press of nature around her. Wild flowers bobbed in the breeze along the shoreline and trees burst with new greenery. She stopped part way through the day to eat and do some fishing. She was rewarded with a trout for dinner.

At home she fileted the fish and got two nice pieces for dinner. She dredged the pieces in flour and fried them in butter and lemon. Along with rice and a salad she savoured this first catch of the season.

Clean-up done, Jess kicked back on the couch in her small apartment, a cup of tea at her side. She couldn't help reliving the last interview with Dr. Adam. How it must have hurt to hear about Hugh McCleery, if, in fact, he didn't know before that. His shock seemed authentic. Of course, that could just be her. She had to go easy on the soft heart in policing.

She turned on the television and settled into a British detective mystery. The British did them so well. She pulled an afghan over her feet and was thoroughly into the plot when the phone rang. It was an "unknown caller." She shouldn't answer it but, she did.

"Hello."

There was silence on the other end followed by breathing noises.

"Who is this? Do you need help?"

More breathing now joined by moaning. The meaning of the call was clear.

"Get off my phone, pervert!" She jabbed the phone off and found that weak response so unsatisfying that she was tempted to throw it. Her own breathing had quickened now along with a spike in her heart rate.

Damn the perverts! Between the phone calls and prowlers she could get spooked if she allowed it. But that wasn't going to happen. She was a police officer who could look after herself. She shouldn't have answered the phone – she knew better and now, being alone, she considered the benefits of company. She wasn't being wimpy, really, just a bit lonely. She picked up the phone and punched in Todd's number.

"How would you like to come over for coffee? Or, I've got some wine. Your choice." Her heart rate returned to normal as she put the white wine on ice.

Adam Chandler's house now acted as if in mourning. There was a somber pall over everything they did. Kelly and Meena wandered aimlessly from one room to another, Meena having trouble controlling tears.

Adam had resigned himself that Aimée was no longer alive or she would have contacted him. Also it made no sense to believe she was with another man. Regardless of how she might be feeling about her marriage, she never would have left her practice in limbo like that. It was obviously the opinion of the police that Adam had killed her. It was the opinion of many people.

He couldn't fight the beliefs of others. The public had made their feelings known with anonymous phone calls, allegations in social media and vandalism at the Chandler home. Social media was especially hard on him. The exchanges ran along the same lines as the official analysis, that the husband was to blame. Isn't it always the husband? they said.

Kelly and Meena were crushed that their daughter's life had been reduced to that of murder victim, that hope had vanished. They tried to keep up their spirits with Adam while all the time an uneasy sense of "what if he…" hung around the edges of their feelings. Meena needed someone to blame. Adam was an easy target.

"If she had affairs with other men it was because she was unhappy in the marriage," Meena said. Tension in the house was high as the days dragged on and nothing was resolved. "Who made her unhappy? You, Adam. You're the other half of the marriage and have to take the blame."

Adam had always liked Kelly and Meena and had enjoyed many visits with them. It was a tremendous blow when Meena turned on him.

"I love Aimée, still love her even with what I know. I tried my best to make her happy. Somewhere it went wrong."

"You don't say," Meena's sarcasm hit Adam where it hurt.

They were sitting in the living room, dinner finished, drinks in hand. A lot of alcohol had disappeared since Aimée went missing. It provided the needed numbing effect for all of them.

"Meena, I'm not going to defend our marriage to you. You don't know what Aimée's been like the last couple of years, so restless, sometimes erratic, but solid enough when it came to her work. But this, what is happening now, has nothing to do with that. Something awful has happened to her, something I've had no part in."

"We only have your word on that," Meena said.

Adam stood up. "My word should be golden with you. But, obviously it's not." He breathed a heavy sigh and faced Kelly. "I don't think this is working anymore. Nothing's being accomplished here. I think it's time for you two to go home. We are only destroying each other. I have no wish to do that."

Kelly stood. "Destroying each other! It's you! She's our daughter!"

"And she's my wife." There was steel in his voice.

"Okay," Kelly said rising to the rhetoric, "if that's how you feel. We'll go in the morning."

"That's how I feel. I wish we could be supportive in this situation. Obviously not. You've let the court of public opinion win. I deserve better than that."

"Do you?" Meena said.

Adam glared at Meena. "I think we're finished here."

Meena and Kelly put down their drinks." "I'm sorry it came to this," Kelly said. "Now, we need to pack." They left the room.

Alone in the room Adam refreshed his drink. The oblivion he sought every day couldn't come soon enough. Tomorrow morning, with Kelly and Meena gone, he would be on his own again. He couldn't wait. The world had crashed in on him and it was time for solitude.

God, he was tired. He had to isolate himself for a while. He felt in step with Aimée's desire to leave all the pressures behind. Suddenly he understood her. He needed, needed, some solitude of his own. Somehow, somewhere, he'd find it.

PART 2

THREE YEARS LATER

CHAPTER 9

When Jessica Morell finally opened her eyes, head above water, her head throbbed with a pulse keeping pace with her racing heart. Her eyes resisted opening, the gravitational pull fighting with her will to pull herself upward away from the river bottom. When she won the struggle and gained the river bank, all she could see was bush, shrubs, trees, a rock outcropping by her right hand. She pulled herself to sitting, clothes soaked and clinging to her, shoes weighted by water. And she was cold; a light breeze rippled over her body causing her to shiver from the mountain-fed river water. Her eyes went to her swollen and bruised left hand, also throbbing. She lifted it with difficulty. It was painful to form a fist, and she suspected one of the bones was broken. She groaned, her right hand going to her head in a reflex designed to ease the pain. Pain came from an egg-sized lump on her temple which she probed carefully. Her fingers came away bloodied.

With that, Jessica's mind fixed on the accident. It had all happened so fast. One minute she was paddling down the river enjoying the outing and suddenly swirling eddies took control of the canoe, overturning it and thrusting her into the freezing water. She'd hit rock as the whirlpool pulled her down before fighting her way to the surface. The canoe had disappeared in the churning wash and was quickly out of sight. She was swimming for her life against the pull of the water, struggling to reach safe ground. With her good hand she'd grabbed a bush overhanging the river and pulled herself ashore where she collapsed with exhaustion. She laid there, chest heaving to collect air. She figured she'd passed out for a few minutes then awakened to a throbbing head and injured hand.

She was alone. Alone in the bush with injuries and disoriented by the accident. She had lost all the supplies packed into the canoe. Her GPS, cell phone, food, tent, her gun.

She eased herself to standing. Everything ached but she had to move on before it got dark. She looked around, gauged the sun's position, and with the river basically running north and south, made her decision and began walking. Enormous pines towered overhead while the ground was dense with undergrowth causing abrasions to her arms and face as she made her way forward. Avoiding bear scat she kept alert to danger, her mind wondering whatever she would do if a bear appeared. She had no defenses. Eventually the sun dried her clothes and she was sweating from her exertions by the time she came to a clearing.

In front of her was an old cabin, small, and dirty with leaves and pine needles. The log walls had moss chinking in some spots. But the windows were clean and bright. The porch creaked under her feet. The clean windows were the only sign of life but she knocked to make her presence known to anyone who might be inside. She called hello but there was no answer. Jessica tried the door which opened to her touch. The structure had only one room large enough to accommodate a cot in one corner that was covered by a sleeping bag and a colourful patchwork quilt draped over the foot. A counter with water bucket and jars of dried food made up a rudimentary kitchen. The half-full jars contained dried peas and beans, pasta and rice.

Someone lived here.

She startled at the sound of footsteps on the porch and turned towards the open door. Silhouetted against the lowering sun was a large, muscular man whose height almost touched the frame. In one hand were two skinned and dressed rabbits, in the other a bloodied knife. Jessica emitted a soft gasp.

"Who are you? What do you want?" the man said. His voice softened as he stepped through the doorway and saw Jessica's injuries. "How did you get here? What happened?"

"I walked, from the river. My canoe overturned."

He stared at her taking in the situation. Jessica stared back, on alert, assessing the potential for violence. She took a step back. He was huge in the room. He wore jeans and a blue quilted jacket. With a brown beard that reached down his chest and brown shoulder-length hair falling over his face, he was through and through a bushman.

"Then you must be tired," he said, "and cold," he added. "Here, have a drink of water then I'll make some tea. Sit over there," he said pointing to the only kitchen-style chair in the room and handing her a glass of water. He flung the naked rabbits onto the counter.

As he faced her and spoke, Jessica was struck by the notion that she had met him before. She wondered about the familiarity she felt in his presence. She wondered how long he had lived here in the woods in a rundown cabin and hunting for his food. She wondered if he would tell her if she asked.

"My name's Jessica Morell," she said. "Thank you for this help." She cradled her injured hand with the other. Her eyes moistened with pain and relief that she wasn't outdoors somewhere curled up beside a log waiting for morning to come.

He lit the flat-topped wood-burning stove, added more kindling and set a pot of water to boil. "Tea will take some time." He noticed her guarding her bruised and swollen hand. "Maybe you'd like to soak that in cold water." He didn't wait for her to agree just poured water into a pan and brought it to her. "Let me clean up that wound on your head." With gentle strokes he cleaned the blood away with disinfectant he had taken from a first aid kit. He finished with a cool cloth, then, carried on over the abrasions on her face. It felt wonderful.

"Thank you," she said, "that feels so much better." She waited a beat. "What's your name? I'd like to be able to thank you properly."

"No need for that," he said. "I'm just some guy in the woods." He wasn't going to elaborate; she could see that as he turned away.

"I'm going to cut up the rabbits for frying. You can lie down if you want to," he said indicating the cot. "Just don't touch the quilt."

"I'm fine. Thanks for your concern." She took a measure of him and said, "I won't touch the quilt." She put the pan of cold water on the counter and retreated to the chair.

She saw him sizing her up. She must be a wild sight, disheveled after her swim, with her dark ponytail coming undone and dirt and debris clinging to her clothes. She was lean with muscular arms from a fitness routine required for work and leisure activities but, she would be no opposition to this strong man. A moment of panic seized her. She knew that wasn't going to help her situation and made an effort to relax, rolled her shoulders and breathed in and out slowly. It didn't seem like he was going to hurt her. Quite the contrary with his competent and gentle ministrations to her injuries.

"I think your hand would feel better if it was wrapped. I have a tensor bandage if it's okay with you." He took the elastic wrap from the first aid kit and held it in his hand to show her what he meant. She nodded agreement. It did help a lot, taking the strain of the injury off the muscles and immobilizing any bone damage.

"Thank you. That really helps."

"Here's your tea," he said stepping in front of her with a mug in his hand. "I only have powdered milk if you want some, but there's sugar."

"Black's fine, thanks."

Back at the counter he picked up the knife and began sectioning the rabbits. He worked with skill and concentration. It was obvious that he had been doing this a long time. Jessica sipped her tea and studied the man. Here was a man living in the back woods adapted to a pioneer style and seemingly content. What was he doing here? It was a difficult lifestyle choice. Then again, maybe he found contentment in the simpler life, no modern conveniences but also no modern headaches. He didn't have to contend with traffic or technology or clashes of temperament with moody peers. Too, he probably was isolated from politics and tragedies that grip the headlines. It has its appeal, she thought. That's why camping and canoeing filled her days off work which took her into contact with the most quarrelsome, angry, disreputable people in society, not to mention dangerous.

The woodsman continued working. He floured the rabbit pieces and put them in oil in a sizzling frying pan on the stovetop. He set some rice to cook. The more Jessica thought about his life here, the more she admired it. The only stumbling block she could think of was the lack of running water. It was fine camping and doing without for a few days at a time but she couldn't see it long term. She liked some conveniences in her life.

"You seem very comfortable with this life," she said.

"It suits me," his back to her as he hovered over the stove.

"Have you been here long?"

"Long enough to be comfortable," he said not turning around. His demeanor didn't invite questions and Jessica kept the rest of her queries to herself.

He let their dinner cook. The sun was low in the sky and Jessica began wondering about finding her way to a road that would lead to rescue.

"It will be dark soon. Am I far from a road that will take me to a town?"

"Too far to start out at this time of day. You wouldn't be picked up hitchhiking if you left now. Where did you come from?"

"I parked my Jeep at Hawksnest Landing just north of Cranbrook. I need to find a way back to it."

"Well, you're here for the night. I can lead you to the road in the morning," he said. "Will you be missed? I mean, is there anyone waiting for you to come home?"

"No. I live alone," she said. Damn. She shouldn't have said that. No one would miss her until she had to return to work. She suddenly felt vulnerable. She had to put her trust in this man who wouldn't share his name or circumstances. She had to spend the night here alone with this stranger. Well, she had defensive skills and would use them if necessary.

Jessica thought he really did seem familiar. Something about his voice and eyes. He wasn't too old, maybe fortyish. Hard to tell with his weathered skin and all that facial hair with only a few grey strands in it. Could he be someone they'd arrested? Did he recognize her? Is that why he wouldn't say his name?

Cooking finished, he added some hot canned tomatoes to the mound of rice on each plate. One plate was almost overflowing with food. He was a big man who needed a lot of fuel. The guy-in-the-woods handed her the other plate.

"Wait," he said. "I'll put the chair at the counter for you." She rose and he shifted the chair's position so that she could manage better. "Pick up the rabbit with your good hand, unless you want me to cut your food." He grinned. Well, maybe he had a sense of humour.

She gave him a wan smile. "Thanks. This looks delicious."

He sat in a webbed lawn chair made comfortable with two pillows. They ate in silence; he devoured what was on his plate and went back for seconds. She didn't realize how hungry she was until the food hit her stomach. She finished her plate then sat back in the chair.

"Why won't you tell me your name?"

She saw him flinch then look up at her. "I don't like labels." He waited a beat. "Okay, if it makes you feel better, you can call me Bruce," he said with a glint in his eyes.

"Ha! What makes you think I'll believe that?"

"You don't have to." A smile creased his face.

"You don't look like a Bruce."

"So sometimes labels are wrong, aren't they?" It was almost a challenge.

"Yes. Sometimes they are."

The sun had fallen in the sky and the light in the cabin had become quite dim. When Bruce finished his second plate of food he put the empty plate on the counter and took two candles from a shelf. He lit them both. He took a lantern from the shelf above the cot where a row of books were held upright with rock bookends. He handed her the lantern.

"There are facilities out back. This is an LED lantern. Take it with you."

"Oh, thanks."

Around the back of the cabin a well-worn path led to an outhouse set back in the trees. She passed a garden plot that looked freshly turned, small green shoots just piercing the surface. There was a pump off to the side of the house. Well good, he had to have a water source.

In the outhouse she set the lantern on the floor then struggled with one hand to manage her clothes. She still had a headache and her injured hand throbbed. She sat for a few moments considering her untenable situation. She had to put in the night in this cabin and there was nothing she could do about it.

Back inside, the kitchen and cooking area had been cleaned up. The man had moved the sleeping bag onto the floor. On the cot were two heavy coats that were meant to be used as blankets. The colourful quilt was folded and placed on the chair, not to be touched.

"Out here I sleep and rise with the sun." He offered her a bottle of Tylenol. "Do you need a couple of these?"

"Oh, yeah. I would appreciate that." He unscrewed the cap for her and offered two pills along with a glass of water. She swallowed them gratefully.

"The cot's for you. I'm fine on the floor."

"Oh, but…"

"It's okay. I'm used to roughing it. I'll sleep just fine." There was a finality to his words. He watched her climb onto the cot and spread the coats over and around her. When she was settled he blew out the two candles. She laid there uncertain about her ability to sleep. She heard him arrange himself in the sleeping bag. Then, before trust deserted her, she slipped into a deep sleep.

CHAPTER 10

JESSICA HEARD THE MAN, SO-CALLED Bruce, moving around the cabin before she saw him. She had slept heavily after her ordeal and her eyelids resisted opening. Having accomplished that, she could see why her feet were cold. The coats as blankets had slipped and exposed her sock-covered feet. She drew them back to the warmth. With a small movement of her head she saw the man standing beside the stove stirring a pot of something. She realized she was famished and sat up too suddenly for her injured head. Her vision blurred and pain returned. His back was to her as she sat there for a moment. The pain subsided and vision became clear enough to see that it was heavy with fog outdoors.

"Oh, no! Will I be able to go home in that?" she said pointing to the window.

He jerked around at her voice, surprised she was awake. "How's your head?" he said. The lump on her temple had turned purple-black and had started travelling down her face. "You really did a number on your head. Are you dizzy or have blurred vision?" Now he was looking at her with concern. Jessica hesitated to answer. He noted the hand to her head and the deep darkness to her eyes. "I'll take that as a yes. You have a concussion. Let me check something." He took the lantern from the shelf and lit it. "Put a hand over your eye for a few seconds. Then open it. I'll shine the light in your eye." She did as she was told.

"Are you a doctor or something?"

He didn't answer but saw her pupil constrict with the light. He followed the same steps with the other eye.

"Your pupils look okay. But I don't think you should go anywhere today." He set the lamp aside and returned to the stove and stirring the pot, took a bowl from the shelf.

"You mean stay here with you?" Her tone was incredulous.

"You should rest with a concussion," he said reasonably.

"You didn't answer me. Are you a doctor?" Her look was penetrating.

"I used to play sports. Everyone picks up some knowledge along the way." He spooned oatmeal into bowls, added a scoop of sugar to each.

"I can't stay here. I have to get back."

"You may not have a choice. Look at the fog. It would be the height of foolishness to start out into the bush in this." He handed her one of the bowls.

Jessica blinked at the outdoors, knew the wisdom of

what he was saying. She just didn't like it. There were far too many ifs in the situation starting with "what if he…?" Her mind went to the possibilities. What if he kept her here against her will? What if he attacked her? What if he raped her? On the other hand she could defend herself. She had the training but perhaps not the strength right now. Obviously she was watching too many psychological thrillers on TV. She had to accept that she was stuck for now and had to let things play out.

She took the bowl of hot cereal and smiled a thank you.

She liked the way he moved across the room, kind of slow and deliberate, like he was comfortable in his skin and surroundings. But then, he'd said that hadn't he. He'd lived like this long enough to be comfortable. She ate the oatmeal cereal with gusto; she was hungry and snickered inwardly at the thought of Oliver Twist asking for "more, please". It was a silly thought that seemed more appropriate for a safe and secure situation, not stuck in the woods with a huge, hairy, bushman.

Just as that thought had crossed her mind, the bushman, Bruce, took the few steps across the room with the oatmeal pot in his hands. She startled and hugged the bowl into her chest as if expecting him to take it from her.

"Might as well eat it all. It doesn't keep well." He spooned more cereal into her bowl and finished it off in his. He proffered sugar which she took and they continued to eat in silence.

Her gaze went to the outdoors again as if the fog

might have dissipated in the last few minutes. With a sigh she saw that it hadn't.

Bruce saw the sigh. "You know, the fog will probably lift by midday if you insist on leaving. I'd advise against it because of your injuries, but, it's your choice." He gave her a steady look.

"You think I can get a ride to town? Is it Charlotte Ridge that's closest?"

"Yeah, Charlotte Ridge. There are always cars and trucks going by throughout the day. Eventually you'd be picked up."

"Okay. If the fog lifts, I'd like to go. I need to get back."

"Suit yourself." His tone told Jessica that she was making a mistake, but she couldn't see herself staying here. Even though he had been kind to her, the "what ifs" continued to circle through her mind. She checked the fog again. It had become a soggy day. Curls of mist left leaves wet and dripping. She should feel lucky she was indoors with a warm fire. So, okay, she did feel lucky. She was so confused about her situation with "Dr. Bruce".

"I don't have any eggs left. I use them quickly when I buy any. But you can have rabbit if that suits. It's outside hanging high away from scrounging animals."

"I'm fine, thanks. Maybe later."

"Sure." He gathered the dishes and put them in a pan with water to soak. "I'm going to do some stuff outside for a while." Removing a deck of cards from the shelf he offered it to her. "This will help pass the time."

He took one of the coats from the cot, added a toque over his abundant hair and left her alone.

She exhaled. Without his presence she could think more clearly about leaving or staying. But she had decided to leave hadn't she? She had a life to get back to, not the least of which was her job. Her three day weekend was over. If she didn't show up tomorrow her boss would send out a search party. The whole detachment would be looking for her. She didn't want to create any more drama than had already happened. She resolved to leave as soon as the fog lifted.

She heard the chunk of an axe hitting wood. One of his many necessary tasks for living off the grid. What kind of a man takes on the hardships of living isolated and without electricity and running water? One who is fed up with the world? Or who has been driven from it? Or is hiding from something? The notion that he was familiar came back to her. Where had she seen him before? In her personal life or professional? She could, in a blunt no-nonsense way, ask him. But, he seemed in every way like a man who guarded his privacy. He'd never answer her. Bruce, indeed.

Without him to see her she reached out and ran her hand over the beautiful cotton quilt that couldn't be used. It was an enigma. Surely there was a story.

The chopping continued outside. She set aside the cards and got up. She didn't feel dizzy which encouraged her to keep going. She needed to use the facilities outdoors. Her down vest had been soaked yesterday but today was dry with the help of the wood stove.

She shrugged into it and opened the door. Moving around the corner of the cabin she came to the garden and woodpile. The woodsman was chopping and didn't notice her approach. Each swing of the axe was powerful, the man putting his muscled shoulders into the movement which he accomplished with a fluid rhythm.

She watched for a minute frankly admiring his prowess, the strength in his arms and back. She could see the muscles rippling with each swing of the axe. Her breath caught as she followed the arc of each movement. He seemed made for this life. Or maybe the rugged life had shaped him as the requirements of the everyday situation landed on him.

Who is this man?

She moved slightly and he caught a glimpse of her from the corner of his eye. He stood straight with the head of the axe resting on the ground.

"I… need to use the facilities," she said gesturing to the outhouse.

"Sure. Go ahead."

She finished in the outhouse and, after struggling with her clothes again, entered the garden area.

"Do you mind if I look around? You know, have a look at where I am?"

"No, if you feel like it. Just don't wander into the bush. Stick to this area." She nodded and walked around the cabin. If he didn't mind her wandering out of his sight, well, he may be big and powerful but probably had no criminal designs on her. She took a breath and relaxed her shoulders.

The fog wasn't as dense now. Birds appeared pecking at the ground, gathering nesting materials. She could see the stand of trees beyond the cabin. She stood still and turned three hundred and sixty degrees taking in the cabin and the small clearing around it. She started to feel the attraction of a remote cabin in the woods, the peace it could bring, surrounded by nature, no TVs, no cell phones or traffic, just quiet.

To the left of the cabin the bush had widened into a path. She followed it for about ten metres. Found that it had been trampled relatively flat. This must be the way out. Her spirits lifted. He'd told her to stay close and she stopped to consider her situation. It was still foggy but that was lifting. She turned back to the cabin. She certainly didn't want to get lost in the dense bush. But, she had a way out, as soon as it was clear enough. Relief swept over her.

Back at the cabin she heard action at the pump followed by Bruce approaching with a pail of water. His face glistened with sweat from his exertions.

"If you want to wash up I can heat some," he offered.

"I'm okay like this." She gestured to the pathway. "Is that the way to the road?"

"Yeah. It's about a thirty minute walk." His brow creased as if to discourage any thoughts she had about leaving.

"Good. I hope the fog disappears fast." She noted his expression and chose not to say anything more.

"There's still coffee," he said. "Maybe you'd like another cup."

"Uh, yes. That sounds good." She followed him into the cabin. It was warm and cozy with a small fire still burning in the stove. He placed the pail on the counter, added some water to the coffee pot and said, "It'll just be a minute."

They studied each other, their eyes meeting and darting away again, each feeling awkward but still interested in knowing the other.

"I think the coffee's boiling," she finally said.

"Yes, you're right. Don't burn yourself." He handed her a steaming mug. They sipped for a few silent moments then Bruce said, "Maybe we should unwrap your hand and see how it is today."

"Okay." She held it out to him, her other hand still holding the mug. He unwrapped it slowly handling her injury gently, a strange sensation against the thick calluses on his hands. Her hand remained swollen and purple. He turned it to look at all areas.

"Try to make a fist. Slowly."

She winced with pain but managed to move all fingers. As he held her hand, one could say he caressed it he was so gentle, small twinges of electricity moved up her arm and into her stomach. It was the injury of course. Certainly not any kind of an attraction to this hairy woodsman. That was a ridiculous thought. But, why did her other hand tingle too? She shoved these erotic thoughts into the back of her mind and moved to withdraw her hand from his. He held it indicating the bandage.

"You'll be more comfortable with it," he said. "I don't think you could move like that if anything was broken," he said re-wrapping the tensor.

"Are you sure you're not a doctor? You seem to have the touch."

"Sure. Dr. Bruce. That's me." He tossed off the remark with a grin. He went to the stove and poured more coffee. "I think you should rest. Read or play cards. I'm going to read for a while." He picked up a brightly covered murder mystery and retreated to the lawn chair. "Take your pick from the shelf," he said indicating his supply of books.

Jessica perused the collection held upright with rocks as bookends. His taste ran to mysteries. They had either been well read or he bought them used. One book, *Walden,* by Henry David Thoreau caught her eye. Of course he would have a copy of *Walden,* that 1854 treatise on finding the simple life in the woods. She lay on cot and thumbed it. Minutes passed into an hour; she dozed off only to waken when he added more wood to the stove.

"Sorry if I disturbed you. I think you needed the sleep."

She roused on her elbows and glanced outside. "The fog's gone! It's safe to head out that path!"

"If you want to. If you have to." His tone spoke volumes.

She stood. He had placed a coat over her legs while

she slept. "I hope I've been as much company as bother to you. I guess it could get lonely out here."

"I'm selective about my company."

"And I passed the admissions test?"

He didn't answer her, just passed to her the down vest that was hers and opened the door. "You'll be there in lots of time to hitch a ride."

"Is that how you get to town? Hitchhiking?"

"A method as old as time."

He led the way and she kept pace behind him. Spring growth had narrowed the path and the woodsman bent off branches of shrubs to open the way as they passed. Jessica looked around trying to pick out markers along the way. One moss-covered rock looked like another, no bush stood out to proclaim "this is the way". The path was clear enough when he showed the way but on her own she would have been lost. *Could* have been lost. She wasn't totally inept in the bush.

A clearing opened in front of them, a highway running ahead, dark asphalt glistening from the early fog.

"You're not far from civilization now." He pointed across the road. "Go to the other side and wait for a ride. It'll take you to Charlotte Ridge."

She found it hard to say goodbye. He had probably saved her life. She held out her hand; he took it, held it a moment longer than necessary. "I wish there was some way I could thank you. But there really isn't. If you find yourself in Cranbrook and need something, look me up." She related her cell number. The phone was gone but perhaps her number could be saved. "Or you can find me at the RCMP detachment. Just ask for Constable Morell." She smiled and left him, walked across the road and took up her place to hitchhike.

He nodded acknowledgement. "I'll wait on this side until you get picked up," he said. He turned and entered the trail and was soon obscured by the brush. Her eyes searched for him without luck, but, she could tell he was there.

The sun was warm, now, on her face. It felt good against the bruising; her head didn't ache anymore. She'd stood by the roadside for a long time, she figured it was half an hour, when a tow-truck hauling a car by a cable came towards her. She stuck out her thumb in hitchhiker fashion and the truck came to a stop beside her. The side door bore the name of A. Rymes Garage and Towing.

"Are you okay, lady? You look kind of battered." The driver wore a Canucks jersey topped by a down vest and grease-stained ball cap. A patchy brown beard dotted his face. He leaned over to the passenger door and opened it.

"I can use a ride," Jess said grasping the door handle. She raised a hand over the roof of the truck, waved and called out to her invisible watcher, "Thank you, Dr. Bruce." She slid into the seat.

"Who the hell is Dr. Bruce?" He turned to the window and searched the bush.

"The guy who lives in there. He rescued me when I had my accident."

"Don't know no Dr. Bruce," he said. "But you sure look like you need rescuing," he said checking out her looks. He accelerated down the road.

"Are you A. Rymes?" she asked.

"No. That's my pa, Auggie. Name's Keith. I work with Pa at the shop." Jess vaguely remembered meeting him before. In connection with a case?

"Thanks for the lift," Jess said. "I've been lucky to find helpful people in the last two days."

"When you live rural you have to watch out for each other. We help each other and can be very caring when we want to," he said moving his hand to Jess's knee where he massaged it showing her how caring he could be. She took his hand firmly and removed it.

"Keep it to yourself, Mr. Rymes," she said sternly.

"Ah," he said as he returned his hand to her knee. "We could have some fun." Without hesitation she grabbed his middle finger and bent it backwards.

Keith Rymes howled and jerked his hand away. "Hey! You got no call to do that! I was just being friendly."

"Without my permission, Mr. Rymes. That could be called assault. Are we clear?" Her tone was firm with traces of anger.

"Yeah, yeah." He was resigned and disappointed. "Just looking for a little fun. Without those bruises you wouldn't be half bad looking."

"Look elsewhere," she said scowling at him. "Just keep driving."

The tense atmosphere in the truck cab lasted the rest

of the silent trip, a thankfully brief drive to Charlotte Ridge. Keith Rymes pulled into the garage lot and Jess got out of the truck. "I need to use your phone to ask someone to come and pick me up."

"Use away, bitch" he mumbled indicating the office with a sweep of his arm.

Jess was only minutes inside. On the way out she waved a thank you to Keith Rymes but was careful to keep it from being friendly.

Charlotte Ridge was a small town; one of those rural outposts that used to be the shopping hub for trappers, miners and farmers. There was less activity these days than a century ago but an elementary school, first aid station and a few shops and cafes kept the town alive for people who preferred country living. The anchor for the town was Nilsson's General Store. In the old fashioned retail tradition, you could get everything there from shoelaces to matches to hammers and nails, milk and bread. Most locals did large shopping trips to the nearby city of Cranbrook but Nilsson's supplied the everyday needs.

Jess crossed the road at the corner, drawing looks from her appearance as she went. She knew she looked beaten so smiled at passersby assuring them of her wellbeing. On entering Nilsson's store, Flo, the owner, glanced towards the tinkling signal at the doorway and did a double-take.

"Jess! Jessica! Is that you? Whatever happened?"

Flo's round and doughy body was encased in a plaid flannel shirt topped by a bibbed apron imprinted with the name of the store, established in 1942. Flo's grandmother had started the store during the Second World War when her husband was away serving in the armed forces in Europe. Flo had grown up with the store and started serving the community herself when she was sixteen, five decades earlier. She loved her job. And if anyone had a question related to the history of Charlotte Ridge, all you had to do was ask Flo.

"Hi, Flo. Yeah, I can't believe it either." By this time Flo's grandson, Zander, had joined them, whistled softly when he saw Jess's face and listened intently to her story.

"I can drive you to your car," Zander offered. Zander was twenty-one-years-old and intent on taking over the store when Flo had had enough. He was tall and lanky with black hair and eruptions on his face. He too wore a Nilsson's apron.

"Thanks, Zander, but it doesn't help. I lost my keys along with everything else in the river so a colleague in Cranbrook is going to my house to get the spare set. He's meeting me here and he'll take me to my car." Flo and Zander nodded.

"You poor thing," Flo said reaching out to touch Jess's arm.

"I'm pretty good now. When it happened I felt like hell but I had help from the guy called Bruce who lives in the bush. Big guy, long brown beard."

Flo and Zander looked questioningly at each other.

"I don't know any Bruce," Flo said. Zander was shaking his head. "Lots of the locals who are bush-rats show up here at some point. All have beards. Mostly like to keep to themselves. Great that he helped you, though."

"Yeah. I'm grateful."

Zander went off to serve a customer while Flo invited Jess to sit beside the counter while she worked. Jess's ride was soon there.

Todd Henley wore his RCMP uniform with squared shoulders like he was starched into place for a photo for a recruiting poster. Everything about him was crisp, some said rigid. There was one memorable incident that was still talked about around the detachment that took the starch out of his demeanor. He'd been mercilessly ribbed for days, lost every speck of his dignity, when he had to help round up some cows loose on a highway and in a neighbor's yard. Frighten a cow and you get a foul purge, foul and sloppy. Frighten a herd and you're swimming in brown muck that becomes a slip and slide. The squad thought it was hilarious, thought he was going to have a breakdown over it, his whole up-tight demeanor destroyed. For days he related the details of the scouring necessary to eliminate the stink. It was his greatest humiliation.

There was nothing starchy about his feelings for Jess. He scoped out the environment, nodded stiffly to Flo then his gaze fell on Jess and he quickly came to her side.

"Jess, my God, you really did a number on yourself." He took her chin in his hand and examined her face. Jess pulled back from his touch. She kept Todd at a distance in her work life, didn't want their private life to be fodder for gossip.

"What about your hand? What do you think?"

"I think it's just badly bruised. I can drive my car if that's what you're asking."

"Yeah, I sort of was."

"Well, let's go. I really want to get home and change clothes."

"I'll bet you do." Jess filled him in on details of her ordeal as they made their way out of the store. With goodbyes to Flo and Zander they left for Hawksnest Landing where Jess's ageing Jeep Wrangler waited.

CHAPTER 11

WITH THE WORST VACATION WEEKEND of her life behind her, Jess walked into the RCMP detachment on Monday morning. She was getting used to the shocked expressions from people when they first saw her face, but, feeling well, she assured them all that everything was good. Her Staff Sergeant, Caleb Sturgis probed her fitness for work.

"Should I be asking for a doc's certificate?" Sturgis peered at her.

"I'm doing fine, sir. Only the bruises left." She no longer wore the elastic bandage on her hand and showed him how well she could use it. "See, no problem," she said.

"Okay, but you're riding with Todd for a couple of days. Nothing solo."

"Sure, boss." Sturgis left her to paperwork which was ever present. She finalized her report about a motor vehicle accident she had attended last week and emailed the file to the insurance company. Then, working from her notes on a domestic dispute in which the wife was hospitalized, she created a report for the Crown Prosecutor and emailed it.

At ten a.m. the phone rang and the whole office sat up on alert as they heard the Staff Sergeant use the words "skeletal" and "human remains". A body had been found by a walker with a dog up on Charlotte Ridge behind the town. He told the caller not to let anyone near the site.

"Sir? Who do you want?" Corporal Abel Thayer asked eagerly. He had already picked up his jacket. Nothing this exciting had happened in the district in years.

"Todd and Jess, you're with me. Colleen, put a call into the General Investigation Section and the Forensic Investigation Section in Kelowna. Ask them to stand by. I'll call from the site and fill them in. Thayer and Franks, follow us in the van." The admin assistant, Colleen, picked up the phone to get things rolling.

Jess was quick to respond and her pulse picked up speed. With a swift exit they were all headed towards Charlotte Ridge within minutes.

The access road to the ridge behind the town was packed gravel used by few people. A religious commune called the ridge home but was situated some distance from the incident site, separated by bush and a small creek that flowed into the town. As they made their approach they were greeted by an agitated man with walking poles and a dog barking incessantly.

Staff Sergeant Sturgis introduced himself. "Michael Heath," the man said as they shook hands. Heath couldn't stop moving, shifting his feet and wiping his hands over his face.

"You don't expect to find a body, do you, when you go for a walk," Heath said anxiously. He worked at calming the black Lab whose barking only stopped when Heath paid attention to him.

"He ran into the bush and came back several times. It was clear he wanted me to follow. He wouldn't stop barking," Heath said.

"Point me to what you found," Sturgis said. "Mr. Heath, stay here and hold the dog back." The dog didn't like that and set up another round of barking as his owner put him on leash. Jess and Todd followed behind the Staff sergeant until they came to a spot that had been lightly trampled. Sticking out of the ground was the dome of a skull and several bones that could only be an arm.

"Well, it's definitely a body," Sturgis said.

"Omigod." Jess had seen death before but always in a residence, someone found dead by visitors, an unexpected death, and twice in car accidents. This was different. This was probably intentional. Jess looked up at Sturgis and Todd for their reactions. Sturgis was thoughtful. Did Todd just close his eyes in silent prayer? Is that what she saw? She wasn't aware of that spiritual side to him. It was a surprise. She and Todd were new together as a couple but not so new that she shouldn't know him.

"Must have been quite a shallow grave," Todd was saying.

"Or animals dug at it and the weather beat on it a lot." Sturgis took in the surroundings and ordered everyone back. "Probably not much we can find here but you never know. Henley, secure the area." They walked back from the site, careful to follow their previous footsteps so as not to disturb the area any more than necessary. Sturgis signaled Michael Heath. "Mr. Heath, let's step over to the cars and we can talk."

Leaning against the squad car, Michael Heath had calmed down and the dog, Mack, sat by his side, tongue hanging out still panting with excitement. Heath was a man in his early sixties, dressed for hiking in waterproof clothes and boots.

"Do you come here often, Mr. Heath?" Sturgis nodded to Jess to take notes.

"Less often than some other trails. Now that the snow's gone I've started coming here once in a while."

"When was the last time?"

"Oh, about ten days ago."

"Was the dog with you then?"

"Oh, yes. He's always with me." Heath continued to stroke the dog's head.

"And nothing seemed unusual that time."

"No, but he only goes into the bush if he smells something, more often rabbits or bush rats." Jess watched Heath's demeanor for anything strange or false. The person who finds a body is sometimes the person who put it there. On this first meeting she found Heath credible.

"Do many people use this road?" Jess looked up from her notes and scanned the area.

"I see people sometimes. Other hikers." Mack, the dog, was under control and Heath relaxed against the car.

"Do you know any names? Anyone we could talk to, to get more of a picture of this area?"

"Well, you could start with the commune up the road a couple of miles. They have to use this road every time they want to go to town. But, they're a weird group, let me tell you."

"Yeah, like weird how?" Sturgis frowned with interest.

"You know. One of those religious cults. Long Jesus robes and sandals." Jess looked up at this then wrote furiously.

"Do you see them here very often?"

"Sometimes. Coming and going."

"Have you seen them stop at this spot?"

"No."

"Anyone else you can think of?"

"There're not too many people up this way… but the Goodwin sisters in town know a lot about what goes on. I see them up here sometimes."

"Okay, thanks. We may need to get back to you; give Constable Morell your contact info, and later, someone will take a formal statement from you." Heath nodded and asked if he could go. Sturgis nodded in return.

He was on the phone immediately to the Forensic Section and related what they'd found. Jess watched him, watched Thayer and Franks run a line of yellow tape around the area.

Off the phone Sturgis called out, "We need to tent the site. Forensics will be here in a few hours." He gestured to Jess to help Thayer with the tent then called the detachment for Colleen to find two more officers to stand guard until Sturgis returned with forensics.

Jess felt the tension in the area ratchet up several degrees. This was really happening. She exchanged glances with Thayer who was clearly ramped up about the situation.

"Henley, Thayer, Franks," Sturgis said, "stay here. No one inside the tape. Scour the area outside the tape for anything that could be evidence. Morell, you're with me. No time like the present to visit the commune."

As they drove the road to the commune, the potholes got larger and deeper. Jess's body bounced so much she bit her tongue.

"Next trip up here we take the Jeep," Sturgis said. "This is hellish." He maneuvered the car as best he could.

"Maybe it's time for horseback," Jess chuckled.

"Yeah, we are the Mounties, after all." Sturgis joined in the laugh.

"I was up here once before," Jess said. "It was for a missing person, showing the picture around." Was the skeletonized body that missing person?

"How did it seem? What was your impression?"

"Definitely a strange bunch. Strict, I'd say. Not a lot of tolerance."

"Mmm," Sturgis replied.

The commune appeared in front of them. One building was an old house probably built nearly a century ago, Jess thought. She remembered the rotting wood siding and cedar shake roof that had substantial moss growing on it. There was a wisp of smoke curling from the chimney. She recalled her visit here several years ago, her meeting with the residents.

Several other buildings covered the immediate area. All had board siding and were newer than the house. There was one large, long building that looked like a barn. Chickens. That was it, they kept chickens. A second long building had been built in the last few years. Had they expanded their egg enterprise or was it a dormitory? How does a commune work on a daily basis? Did families live together? Perhaps one building was used as a church. There were five buildings in all and, behind the structures, Jess could see the fenced area that had to be garden. In front of one small building several goats milled about. Brown chickens scratched in the dirt nearby. Definite improvements had been made in the last years.

Sturgis stopped the car at the house and they got out. "Might as well start here," he said.

As they stepped onto the porch the door opened. A man, six feet and thin stood in the entrance. He wore a long beige robe and sandals with wool socks. Thermal underwear peeked out at his ankles. His head and facial hair was shoulder length. He was about forty years old. Jess recognized him as Brother Jedidiah.

"What can I do for you, Officer?" he said, his face creased in a frown. "We don't get many visitors here."

Sturgis took the lead. "I'm Staff Sergeant Sturgis and this is Constable Morell. And you are…?

"Name's Jedidiah, God's blessing."

Jess took in the room. A small room with an old, small kitchen and some seating area. It was heated by a wood stove in the corner. A plaque on the wall asked the Lord to Bless This House. A young woman washed dishes at the sink and didn't let the arrival of police officers interrupt her work. She, too, wore a robe-like garment in gray, long brown hair in a braid. She didn't enter the conversation and only took surreptitious glances in the direction of the door.

"There's a serious situation in the area, sir. We'd like to ask you some questions," Sturgis continued.

"We don't involve ourselves in the secular world, Sergeant. We just try to live a godly life. I can't imagine what we could tell you." He hadn't invited them to step inside. "Are we in any danger? Should I gather the flock together?"

"There's no immediate danger, sir." Sturgis told him of the discovery down the road. "It isn't a fresh grave so we wonder about unusual activity in the area over time. Anything, thinking back on it, that doesn't seem right to you."

Jedidiah put his hands together. "God bless his poor soul," he said. The woman at the sink stopped her washing, closed her eyes and folded her hands in prayer mode along with Jedidiah.

"How many people live here, sir?"

"We have thirty souls here right now. Our numbers change as people come to us or find they can't abide by our rules and leave."

"I'll ask you to talk to your people. Especially the ones who have been here the longest. We'll come back again for any information you can give us. If someone wants to stop into the detachment in Cranbrook, that's fine too. Any help you can give us would be appreciated." He passed Jedidiah a business card. The man didn't look at it, just palmed it and clasped his hands behind his back.

"Good day, Sergeant," he said and closed the door before Sturgis and Morell turned away.

As they got into the squad car Jess asked, "What do you think? Do you trust them?"

"What makes you ask that?" He started the car.

"I don't trust anyone with a single agenda or message. Especially not religious fundamentalists. They seem to fit that description."

"Don't be too quick to judge. Be careful about too narrow a perspective. We're just at the beginning of this investigation." They were back on the pot-holed road.

"Sorry, sir. But people like that always rub me the wrong way. Must be my upbringing."

"We're all shaped by our roots, aren't we," he said. "But, I've always thought that coming to religion later in life is when you get extremists."

"I wonder when those thirty people found the Lord?" Sturgis was right to rein in her thinking. She was green as grass when it came to murder, if that's what it was. Nothing fouls an investigation worse than jumping to premature, unsubstantiated conclusions.

They stopped at the burial site where Sturgis told Thayer and Franks to stay put as guards. Henley could return to the detachment. They'd pull the missing persons files but there wasn't much more they could do until forensics gave them something to work with.

"Jess, when we get back to the barn, run Michael Heath's name and see what you come up with. We need to know as much as we can about all the actors in this tragic play."

CHAPTER 12

THE CRANBROOK SMALL TOWN GRAPEVINE did its job in record time. By the next morning, all the coffee groups were talking about the body found at Charlotte Ridge. In the cafes, at Starbucks, at Tim Hortons the big questions were being asked. Who was the body and who put it there? One conclusion that gained traction was that it was an early settler who had been buried there by family. Crime buffs leaned towards a murder victim, but then, who was missing? Maybe it was a stranger just passing through who had stirred the killer passions of some local. Was there a murderer living among them? Should they start locking their doors?

In Charlotte Ridge, townsfolk watched the forensics vans drive through, some personnel stopping for a take-out coffee before starting the excavation of the body and examination of the site. The locals talked of nothing else, many hanging out at the Nilsson General Store to share the excitement with neighbours. Everyone was tense with pumped-up expectations and usually looked to Flo Nilsson for the latest news. Flo gloried in the role of broadcaster of each nugget of information. But Michael Heath, as finder of the body, stood in the spotlight today.

"It was shocking to find it," Heath said to the group.

"But, what material for your books," Flo offered. Michael Heath was a writer and had two self-published mysteries. With each book he tried vigourously and in vain to interest a commercial publisher in the novels. That was still a fervent goal. Many locals teased him, some not so gently, that they were all characters in his plots.

"Well, I'm always looking for plots," Heath said airily. "Think of the possibilities with an unknown skeleton."

Nods and murmurs all around.

Carl Thurlow, known as Crazy Carl by the less enlightened Charlotte Ridge residents, stood with the same coffee-drinking group that included Michael Heath and the Goodwin sisters, descendants of the town's founder. Carl was medium build with ragged brown hair falling over his ears under a black cowboy hat and boots. Well known for his erratic processing of information and occasional delusions he described to anyone who would listen. Today he was unusually quiet while Heath related his story and Charlotte Goodwin took over from him. That didn't mean Carl's mind was quiet. Visions of death, of souls released to their reward occupied his tangled thoughts. He wasn't listening to Charlotte.

"Sure people died and were buried in the old days wherever they wanted to plant them," Charlotte said with the authority of the longest resident of Charlotte Ridge. "My great-grandfather used to tell about fights and grudges at the mines when guys got all drunked-up then ended with someone disappearing. You didn't see the Mounties in those days, over a century ago, for months on end. This was really frontier country then and lawless to boot."

Charlotte's sister, Joy, nodded in agreement. She tended to defer to Charlotte in all things. Many people, newcomers to the community, thought they couldn't possibly be sisters, Charlotte being heavy and round with wild white hair and a know-it-all personality. Joy, quiet, slim with red highlights in her short cap of hair. Genetics were a mystery.

"You wait," Charlotte continued authoritatively. "They won't be able to identify the remains. Bet they're old as dirt."

"God put them there." Crazy Carl, in denim overalls finally spoke. His eyes gleamed with the excitement of the possessed. "He does things like that. Puts people where He wants them, He does. Should we go see? Can we go see?" he said addressing Michael.

"Uh, sure," Heath said. "Whatever is happening can only add to the story." He turned away dropping his coffee cup into the dirty dish bin.

"Naw, not me," Charlotte said sloughing it off.

"What's the point?" She walked away, Joy following her, to pick up a few groceries.

"I'll go," Auggie Rymes said. "We'll take my truck." He hitched his pants in the signature gesture he affected whenever he made a decision.

Flo Nilsson, standing behind the counter, watched them go and wondered why Auggie, who generally didn't give a damn about Carl, would willingly spend time with him.

Zander Nilsson, also behind the counter beside his grandmother, watched and listened. He didn't need any more trips to the ridge. He didn't need Carl blabbering in his ear or speculation swirling around him about the body. His eyes welled with memories. He thought he knew who the body was – because he could never forget.

He had to tell the cops. He wouldn't let those freaks get away with it.

The next day Jess went to work with some degree of excitement. The inquiry about Michael Heath had revealed that he had two DUIs on his record. He'd lost his license for a period of time because of it. Yesterday he had seemed just like the hiker he appeared, a solid senior that did his duty when it was needed. She wrote up this report before leaving for Charlotte Ridge.

This unknown body was the peak experience of her career to date and she was eager for the hours to come. She had drawn guard and crowd control duty at the site, driving there with Todd Henley at the wheel. They talked little during the ride but Todd suggested they get a drink together after their shift. Jess said, "Sure. We'll probably need one… or two."

Corporal Abel Thayer was left in the office to take the inevitable phone calls, to weed through the ones that had merit and needed follow-up and to dispense with the cranks. When they arrived at the ridge the night shift had gone and Joe Franks was already holding back a handful of lookie-loos. Staff Sergeant Sturgis stood talking quietly with a forensics officer and an RCMP inspector just outside the tape.

The excavation process was slow, the forensics team sifting through soil as they went. The hours passed. Henley was sent for sandwiches and drinks. Jess walked the perimeter of the site, stamping her feet to stimulate circulation after so much standing. The exciting prospects for the day had become tedium. She began putting in time creating murder scenarios in her head. Various people in the crowd that has gathered took the lead in her story. A murder mystery. Her imagination leapt ahead building scenarios as she went, not unlike her favourite BBC dramas.

She picked out that creep, Keith Rymes. He was laughing as if the scene was a comedy routine. No respect for the seriousness of what was unfolding. What was he doing here? Does he know something about the body? The dump site? Her first impression of him was that he was shifty enough to be considered.

Who was that man in the black cowboy hat? He talked earnestly to the man beside him, pulling at his arm to gain his attention. "He dug a hole," he said, "he dug a hole for a body not potatoes." The man pulled away clearly annoyed but didn't leave, almost swatted at the black-hat-man and maintained a deep interest in the surroundings. With his hand to his chin he looked thoughtfully on. Did he know the victim? Maybe he was having an affair with her (her?) but had to kill her when she threatened exposure. Not a bad scenario. Did he look like a murderer?

The commune was represented by their leader, Jedidiah, and another robed man. She had noticed them when they arrived, and a short time later, left. This was close to home for them. Maybe close enough to be party to it? Is there someone they crossed paths with? Someone who wouldn't follow their rules?

Dozens of other townspeople came and went with nothing to see but a tent and taped area. The actual excavation was out of sight, nothing of interest for your average person. Was the murderer among the group? Her imagination had made it murder even if it wasn't official yet. She was eager to get moving on this. Why was it taking so long?

"Why is it taking so long?" someone called out.

"It takes as long as it takes," she answered back. "This has to be done methodically." So, that was the answer.

A very short time later the tent opened and several white-clad personnel walked out into the sunlight carrying a black body bag between them. A hush fell over the crowd, a solemn moment, the climax of their wait finally upon them. No one made a sound until the coroner's van closed its doors and drove away with its tragic contents.

"What can you tell us?" someone shouted.

This set up a chain reaction of shouted questions which the Staff Sergeant quelled with raised hands and response of "Quiet! We can't tell you anything at this time. An autopsy will be done and public statements will follow as appropriate. Now, everyone, please go home. There is nothing to see."

"Are we safe? Are we safe in our beds?" A few people emboldened by this query called out more questions.

"If anyone has any reason to feel they are not safe, come to the detachment and report your concerns," Sturgis said reasonably. "If anyone has any information about this, please come to the detachment and make a statement. That's all, folks. Now, please go home." He instructed the staff that it was still a secure site and left Franks with another constable on guard. Sturgis left with the inspector.

Jess and Todd Henley left together. "Well, what do you think?" Todd said his eyes forward, attention on the road.

"I can't wait for the autopsy is what I think. We don't even know age or sex at this point. Can't do anything unless someone comes in with information." She twisted in her seat for a better angle towards Todd. "But, what I've been thinking all day is that it's murder. Who buries a body out in a spot like that except to hide it?"

Their shift was almost over and at the station they

handed over to the night shift. Jess and Todd agreed to change out of uniform and meet at the Barn Door, their favourite eatery.

At home, Jess showered and changed spending some time examining her face and hand for improvement. Neither was very sore now and the bruises diminishing. She applied some light makeup to hide what she could. Her mind easily drifted to Dr. Bruce. Such an interesting character. He was both strength and tenderness and clearly a survivor. He had the smarts to exist without the supports of the modern world. She had enough camping experience to know the challenges. She admired him… admired him? Who was she kidding? She had felt a pull towards him, like she was actually moving into his space as if he was magnetic and she was helpless to hold back.

When she had a day off she would go and find him, to return the elastic bandage. Certainly she should give it back. One day he might need it for himself, she reasoned. That decided, she left her house for her evening with Todd, an evening that wasn't really a date, and with thoughts of Dr. Bruce lingering in her head.

CHAPTER 13

Over dinner at the Barn Door, it was hard to stay off the topic of the body. The place, designed and decorated with reclaimed wood, was full and guests nudged up against each other, the tables being too close. Cranbrook was a small town; they were recognized, even out of uniform. Jess and Todd knew that careless talk in the wrong place could result in rumours, headlines. The Barn Door was the wrong place. In jeans and puffy vests, they ate juicy quarter-pound burgers and talked about Jess's camping trip instead.

"The first day and night were great. You know, one of those starry nights when everything is still and you sit by a campfire with the moon full and bright above."

"You paint a great picture, Jess. Maybe you and I could do it sometime." Todd looked at her with barbeque sauce on his chin. Jess reached over with a napkin and wiped the red blot from his face. She returned to her burger.

"Maybe. I sure want to. First I have to replace all my equipment. I phoned the insurance agent and she told me to list all that I lost and bring in the list. What a pain. But it really added up, the canoe, GPS, phone, tent, cookware, fishing gear, gun. It's around $4000."

"You were lucky to get back at all. It really is foolhardy to do that kind of thing on your own. Look what happened. You need to be with someone."

Jess understood the wisdom of what he said but bristled at his censoring tone. She'd thought she had herself covered with a GPS and phone. She was lucky to meet Dr. Bruce. It was dead easy to get lost in the bush. The mystery man might actually have saved her life. Now that she was in better shape, she had to go back and find him to say thank you, again. She would wash and return the bandage too. It was the thing to do.

Todd was talking; she could hear the drone of his voice but the words weren't clear. Her mind had filled with an image of the woodsman, his towering frame muscled from hard living, his dark eyes that gentled when he cared for her injuries. She should stop thinking of him as Dr. Bruce and switch to something like... The Gentle Woodsman. That was him, gentle under the rough exterior. The Gentle Woodsman. It sounded like the title to a fairytale.

Todd was telling her about the camping he did as a kid in northern Ontario. "My father and two brothers and I would camp a lot in the summer, weekends when Dad was off. We did our best to miss the mosquito and black fly season. That was fierce. Mom got pretty ticked off with us by the end of summer. We'd missed a lot of church by then."

"Church, huh. My childhood too. Have to admit it didn't take. I don't attend now."

"My family went to a strong evangelical church, no real denomination. Both parents were into it and religion featured in our life all week. Prayer groups, church youth groups, church twice on Sunday and constant reminders to behave as if Jesus might drop in any minute."

"Did you? Behave?" Intrigued.

"Ha! More than you can imagine. We had the fear of God drilled into us. None of us kids was ever 'good' enough." Todd's face fell as the memories surfaced. "If my parents knew about our relationship, I would be condemned to hell," he said quietly raising his eyes to meet Jess's. "Not that I would change anything." He paused. "I'm sorry. I shouldn't have dropped that on you."

Jess flushed at the thought of their relationship. In the last year they had moved from colleagues to friends to lovers. They'd ended up in bed one snowy night when Jess had thrown a party to initiate her new digs, a rental house with lots of room for her outdoor equipment. Todd kept putting off going home, waiting after everyone else had left for the blizzard conditions to improve. Between rum toddies and huddling under a blanket to keep warm in the draughty old house, the boundaries fell and the relationship took the leap into sex.

Todd was a more-than-competent lover. Her body responded to his touch. He kissed and stroked all the right places but she had always felt something not quite committed or happy about him. Now she thought she knew why. Overriding guilt. The knowledge was like an anchor had suddenly shackled her feelings. If what he said was true, she didn't want their extremely pleasurable recreation to be tainted. Didn't want him thinking about childhood lessons of hell and brimstone as part of their lovemaking. They'd never expressed love to each other and he'd never talked about those memories before. She could see now that they were both restrained in their feelings, Todd because the hard childhood lessons were carved deeply into his psyche, Jess because… she didn't know. Those three important little words just wouldn't come.

These revelations explained the prayer-like pose at the crime scene yesterday. Yes, she had really seen it. She had never seen any nuances of religion in him before. How much was he suppressing and what emotions?

He'd become thoughtful; his flow of chatter had drifted into reverie. The reminder of his past had taken him to another place. Suddenly, he was back. "All finished? I put a bottle of wine in the car. I thought maybe we could open it at your place."

"Uh… not tonight, okay? We both work tomorrow and it was a tiring day up on the ridge. I got cold to the bone standing around. An early night, okay? And a raincheck?"

Disappointment crossed his face but he wasn't one to push. "Sure. I understand. The wine will keep."

"Coffee here?"

"What about the café down the street, the one with the thirty-one flavours of ice cream. I could murder a butter pecan sundae."

"You're on."

Another day passed and she'd done four ten-hour shifts and found that bed felt like heaven. She always slept deeply when her shifts were done. She pulled the comforter tightly around her neck and paid no attention to the morning sunshine coming into the room. She lay like that for a few minutes allowing her body to slowly stretch awake.

Then her eyes popped open. Today she was going back to the entrance to the trail to Dr. Bruce's cabin. She'd take precautions using a GPS which she'd purchased in a lunch break yesterday. She had a new cell phone. In addition she'd break branches to mark her path in the old tradition. She had no intention of getting lost. She hadn't told Todd she was going. She hadn't told anyone. It was a move that was exactly what Todd had censored her about. But, Dr. Bruce, or the Gentle Woodsman, was obviously a private man and she wanted to help him keep it that way. She would be fine. She was confident that finding him again was possible. She had taken her bearings with stone markers when she was out on the road and knew where to start.

Showered and dressed she finished her coffee and put the clean tensor bandage in a bag. With a sudden thought she added a few apples, oranges and bananas. Taking fresh fruit to him would be a good way to say thank you. She could even stop at Subway and get a couple of sandwiches with fresh vegetables on them.

Soon on the road it was only a short trip from Cranbrook to Charlotte Ridge where the small town had opened for the day. Coffee shops were bustling. She noticed the man in the black cowboy hat who had been at the excavation walking along, hands waving and talking to himself. He was unkempt with ragged hair. She didn't know much about mental disorders but wondered if he was hearing voices giving messages to him and responding to them. She'd seen him around Charlotte Ridge but didn't know him, didn't think he'd come to the attention of the justice system, at least not in the four years since she had been here. She wondered if he had family, how he managed. Her mind roamed around this topic as she made her way out of town.

A few kilometres along the highway she found the spot where Keith Rymes had given her a ride. It was marked with two large rocks. She pulled to the shoulder, got out with her bags of groceries and locked the Jeep. She walked a few yards up and down the road searching for the opening of the path they had taken. She found a likely spot, locked in the coordinates on the GPS for her return and plunged into the bush.

It was a clear day and the sun shone through gaps in the foliage warming Jess and keeping her optimistically moving forward. The undergrowth was thick around the discernable path but Jess felt she was making progress. Nothing looked familiar. Every tree and bush looked like every other one. She marked her trail with broken branches and checked the GPS. She seemed to walk for a long time but she thought her expectations of coming into a clearing only made it seem that way.

And, then, there was the clearing. The log cabin with its sagging porch open to the sunlight appeared welcoming as it hadn't when she stumbled on it after her accident. Then, it was just a massive relief like a life ring thrown to a drowning person.

She didn't see him. She walked the perimeter of the cabin. He wasn't at the garden and she wondered if maybe he'd gone to town. She rounded the corner to the front again and found him standing at the door.

"I saw a shape go by," he said by way of explanation. He scrubbed a hand over his face. He wore jeans and a plaid flannel shirt. Brown hair and beard still long and, today, unkempt, as if he had just risen from a nap. She supposed he could nap whenever the mood struck him.

"I hope you don't mind me coming back. I wanted to thank you by returning your tensor bandage. You might need it." She held up the bag. "And brought some fresh goodies too. If you haven't had lunch…?"

He brightened at that, suddenly awake and welcoming. "Come in, come in. It's good to see you and see you looking so recovered."

She mounted the porch and followed him into the cabin. Looking around, she saw the beautiful quilt still had a special place draped over the chair. It was always placed somewhere with care. Even though her stay here had been brief, she liked the feel of the place, sort of like returning to a holiday spot. In truth, she *was* returning to her vacation spot, however unorthodox her weekend had turned out. Dr. Bruce was different, a change from her everyday life. This life in the bush was special in its own way. She had never camped for any length of time and wondered about long-term living in the bush.

"I was just about to make coffee." He busied himself at the counter. "I had quite an interrupted sleep last night. There was a bear with two cubs around knocking things about."

"You think they're gone?" Now on alert. She had forgotten to bring bear spray. Dumb, dumb.

"Oh, yeah. They are mostly nocturnal so will be sleeping the early part of the day."

"I could have walked right past them." Jess's arms closed around her chest. How stupid could she be?

"Maybe you did." He threw her a grin. There it was, the glint in his eye the Jess remembered. She broke into a smile.

"Coffee's ready." He filled two mugs.

"So is lunch." Jess took sandwiches from the bag and offered one.

"This is great. As satisfying as a hot shower after a camping trip," he said.

"I get that!" Jess smiled.

"Yeah, I miss the crunch of fresh foods. But I splurge a bit when I go into Charlotte Ridge for supplies."

"Then I brought the right thing," she said holding aloft an orange.

"That's like ambrosia." His smile covered his whole face, even the hairy part she couldn't really see. "That's dessert," he said setting it aside.

They made headway on their sandwiches in silent enjoyment. Their eyes met over top of the food and they took in the sight of each other.

"I didn't think I'd see you again," he said, his voice low.

"I'm glad I found you," Jess replied with sincerity.

"I find you easy to be with," he said, "and I can't say that about many people these days, especially police officers."

Jess bristled. "Why? Or shouldn't I ask that?"

"I find you easy to be with because you're a genuinely nice person. Because you weren't intrusive about my life when you stayed here. Because you have an open face that tells me what you are thinking." He paused. "Because you light up this cabin."

Jess flushed. "Oh. I like you too, enough to want to come back. Should I just forget that you singled out police officers?"

"When you're a scruffy guy with big hair living in the bush you attract attention. I'm always on somebody's radar when I go to town."

"People seem to accept you in town. I asked Flo if she knew Dr. Bruce and she said they have all kinds of bush people coming in. She couldn't place you. You haven't been singled out." Jess finished her sandwich and crumpled the paper. She reached over to take the other paper too when he covered her hand with his. She tensed. His touch sent little shivers through her. She made a move to pull away.

"Don't be afraid. I just want to say thank you for coming back. I think I need more social interaction. I keep really busy here just with survival but sometimes… it would be nice to talk to someone." He removed his hand.

"Well," she said, "I can stay a while. Why don't we play cards? Or do you want to hear news from the outside world? Or," she said mischievously, "you could tell me the story of the quilt."

He laughed and shook his head. "Cards it is," he said. "There isn't much out there that interests me. I don't need to be agitated and stressed like most of the population who listen to the constant media." He rose and picked the deck of cards off the high shelf. "Any favourites? How about gin rummy? Or we could play chess."

"You play by yourself?"

"Yeah. Playing both sides of the board is a challenge."

"My chess is very rusty. Gin rummy suits me." They fell easily into conversation and played with enthusiasm. Both displayed a competitive side. Dr. Bruce told stories about life in the bush. He told them in a self-deprecating style that brought laughter. There was the raccoon standoff, the hovering cougar on the roof, the damn deer that grazed on his garden. "The deer are as graceful as a ballet when they leap a six foot fence into my garden. In the interests of my food supply I had to add two feet to the top of it."

Dr. Bruce poured more coffee and they shared an orange even though Jess protested it was his. It was a warm and convivial atmosphere that became flirtatious as time passed. They smiled a lot finding occasions to touch the other's hand.

Finally, when Jess checked the outdoors, she felt it was time she left before the sun travelled any farther across the sky.

"Thank you so much for coming. It's been a happy day for me," he said putting away the cards.

"Me too," Jess said. "I certainly don't want to push your boundaries but, I could come back to see you again, if you wanted."

He looked into her open, honest face, felt an attraction that was so long absent in his life. He wanted to reach out to her but checked himself. "Yes. I would like that."

Jess put on her jacket and opened the door. Dr. Bruce was right behind her. "I'm coming with you to the road. I've got a bear banger and spray. I want to see you safely to your car."

They followed the path. Jess pointed out the broken twigs. "Who needs GPS?" he quipped.

At the road they stood beside each other while Jess unlocked the Jeep. He took both her hands in his. She could feel the calluses, the warmth.

"I've been thinking," he said, "Next time, would you consider staying the night? Bring a sleeping bag and we could go hunting and I'll show you how to skin a rabbit. It might come in handy on your next canoe trip. Every girl should know how to do it." He stood there, a smile playing around his lips, the tease obvious.

"Dr. Bruce, I believe you are flirting with me." He threw back his head and laughed. He was still holding her hands and she reached and took his forearms to pull him closer. She whispered in his ear, "I'll come back if you tell me your name."

Then, he whispered in hers, "I'll tell you my name *when* you come back."

She turned away, settled into the Jeep, fired it up, and turned towards Charlotte Ridge. She left him by the roadside, their budding undeclared want a tether between them.

CHAPTER 14

"Listen up, guys. The autopsy report is in." Sturgis faced the squad room to make the announcement. "This is what we've got." He paused to look at the papers. "The body has been in the ground two to four years. It's female aged twenty-five to forty. She was about five feet six inches tall with a history of a fractured right humerus; that's upper arm to you; that fracture was several years old at the time of death. The body had sustained multiple fractures at the time of death which include six ribs, pelvis, and both femurs. The pathologist said there would have been massive internal damage. Artifacts found in the surrounding dirt were cigarette butts, which are much more recent than the body, flecks of white paint consistent with that used on a motor vehicle, bits of decomposed clothing, some leather from a black coat, and disintegrating pieces of a blue tarpaulin. There was also a canvas gardening glove. The summary says, 'These findings are consistent with being struck by a vehicle going at speed, then, the body was wrapped in a tarpaulin and buried where it was found.'"

He looked up at the staff taking in his words. They all listened with rapt attention. "This gives us a few things to go on. We are having the paint flecks analyzed for type and model of vehicle it was used on. The glove is being analyzed for DNA. The cigarette butts will be analyzed to see if any DNA remains. That's unlikely with exposure. There are small pieces of clothing, especially the coat fragments, that family members may be able to identify. Abel, I want you and Franks to scour the missing persons' files and come up with possibles. Jess, you and Todd go back to Charlotte Ridge and start questioning anyone that seems the least bit connected. I know that doesn't give you much to start with, but, locals often know more than they are aware of. They have history to draw on. I'll be talking to the repair shops in town, see if anyone brought in a vehicle with damages consistent with this information." He looked over the sea of faces. "Okay, folks, let's give this woman a name." Jess felt a surge of energy. Finally they had something to work with.

Todd Henley signed out a vehicle, an SUV, and, with Todd driving, they were soon on the road to Charlotte Ridge. The morning sky was bright; the storms of the last few days had passed. Todd shot glances at Jess. She had her duty hat in her lap and the sun was hitting the top of her head pulling red highlights from her dark brown hair. It looked like a halo. It gave him the sensation of an angel sitting beside him. It filled him with happiness. They hadn't seen enough of each other in the last few days. It almost felt like Jess was pulling away from him, putting him off the way she did. Maybe, tonight, they could change that.

Finally, he spoke. "What about tonight, Jess? Can we make a plan for dinner and spend the evening together?"

She turned her face to him clearly drawn away from deep thoughts. "Um? What was that?"

"I said, can we get together tonight, dinner and how about Spanish coffees after at my place?"

"Uh, let's wait and see how the day goes, okay? We don't know what's going to come up."

Todd was stung. There. She did it again. She wouldn't commit to a simple evening. It's been more than three weeks since they'd been intimate and each time he tried to plan something, she withdrew. Was he losing her? After all he'd done for her, all he'd done to situate himself into her life, the chances he'd taken in her neighbourhood. He wouldn't let her go. This would work out, he told himself. She was just going through something, maybe left over from her canoe accident. All he had to do was be patient. "Love is patient, love is kind…"

His thoughts travelled along these lines as he drove until Jess finally spoke up. "Let's start at the General Store. That seems to be the community gossip centre so someone might know something." She put her hat back on, sat up straight. Todd could tell she was all business now.

It was mid-morning at the General Store. Flo and Zander Nilsson were behind the counter serving a customer. That man with the black cowboy hat she'd seen at the burial site was sitting alone in the back of the store, rocking his body and muttering about digging and being tangled. A large coffee group was still sitting around. One or two were throwing looks at Crazy Carl. The rest acted like he wasn't there.

"Well, look who's back," Flo said with a big smile. "You look better than the last time I saw you," she said of Jess. "You almost look healed."

"Things are much better. And thanks again for the help the other day. You remember Constable Henley?" They nodded at each other. "Today we need your help again. I'm sure there's been a lot of talk about the body found on the ridge. Maybe people have started to think and remember something that might help us. The body is between two and four years old, female, twenty-five to forty years old. She was wearing a black leather coat." She turned to the coffee group which had stopped talking and all eyes were on the cops. "Does this ring any bells with you folk, being local and all? Anybody come to mind, someone who disappeared around then?"

She was greeted by silence, head shaking. "Any unusual activity in the area back then, transient workers, like construction or road-building?"

"Dig a hole, dig a hole," could be heard from Crazy Carl who had noticed the police uniforms. He stood and shuffled towards the officers. "Dig a big hole for the body." His hands were in constant motion as if digging.

"Carl, is it?" Jess said. "What hole? Who dug a hole?"

Carl's agitation grew; he shuffled and muttered incoherent words except for the word police.

"Who dug a hole, Carl?"

"Police, police dug a hole."

"He was up there on the ridge when they excavated the body," Flo explained. "He gets upset easily. Carl," Flo said coming around the corner of the counter. "Don't bother the officers. Zander, he's really agitated, but aren't we all. How be you take him home. Make sure Bobby's there to look after him."

"Sure, Gran. Right away." Zander reached for his jacket, motioned to Carl. "C'mon, Carl. I'll take you home. We'll have coffee at your place." Carl left easily with Zander.

"Carl's used to being around Zander. They get along fine. Bobby's Carl's brother. He'll settle him down."

"I guess everybody is agitated about the body. It's disturbing," Jess said. "So we need any help you can give us," she said facing the group. "Can you think of anyone we can talk to who might have some knowledge?"

"Well, Flo's the best there is," said Michael Heath. "Also the Goodwin sisters. Go see them. You can see their house from here." He got up and pointed out the window at the small house down the street with three cabins on the lot.

"Okay, thanks." She spoke directly to Heath now. "If you haven't made your official statement yet, perhaps we could come by your house and take care of that."

"Sure. Just down the road from the Goodwins. The grey vinyl."

"Great. Thanks. We'll see the Goodwins then come to your place." She turned to the rest of the coffee group. "If anyone thinks of anything just call the Cranbrook detachment." To Flo she said, "I'll leave a card with you, Flo."

"Right you are," Flo said accepting it.

Outside, Zander Nilsson was waiting at the corner of the porch.

"Can we walk with you?"

"Sure. Anything in particular you want to say? Zander, is it?" Jess said recognizing his need to talk. Carl trailed along behind.

"Yeah, I…uh, know someone who went missing."

Jess and Todd stopped in their tracks.

"You do? Young female?"

"Yeah." Zander was nervous, fidgeting with the button on his sleeve. Carl stood by his side twitching with agitation. "I've never told anyone this; it was a secret between her and me."

"A secret," Carl said. "There's a secret. Secrets make tangles." Zander shushed him.

"Tell us what happened, Zander." Todd took out his notepad.

"I was seeing a girl. They called her Charity. The commune, I mean. Her real name was Mariah Talman. She wandered into Charlotte Ridge about four years ago and ended up in that freaky commune on the ridge. I met her at the store. She told me, at first, she found it peaceful, liked the simple life… but, later she couldn't stand the restrictions. Mainly, that was after she met me."

"So she tried to leave?"

"She wanted to. She told me they would come and find her if she left. They would hurt her, drag her back, attack her and humiliate her. I know it sounds extreme but maybe she was right." He took a big breath. They continued walking and were now outside the Goodwin sisters' place. "Anyway, before she could work out how to leave–you're watched all the time she said and she was afraid of them–we found out she was pregnant." A look of grief crossed his face. "So we made plans for her to come live with me and Gran. We hadn't told Gran yet but it would have been okay." His shoulders slumped. "Anyway, she disappeared. I went to the commune and asked questions, lots of them. I got angry and they told me she had left, just walked away. Like they would allow that," he said bitterly. "They said I was trespassing and made me leave. That Jedidiah guy is a menacing brute."

"And you think this body might be Mariah?"

"It could be, couldn't it? Those commune people are crazy as shit!" Zander face reddened at the thought.

"Did you ever see any signs of violence against Mariah? Like bruises, scrapes or worse?"

"No. And I would have noticed." He blushed at this comment.

"Have you heard about violence against other commune members?"

"Nothing specific except, once, I noticed that wife

of Brother Jedidiah had a bruise on her face. Think she calls herself Sister Judith."

"Anything else?"

"Just that it's pretty well accepted that the members, women especially, are intimidated into staying and put up with harsh treatment. Mariah told me that."

"You've never heard from Mariah since she disappeared? Nothing on social media?"

"No. She gave me her cell phone when she was living there. She wasn't allowed to have it. I can't believe she would just leave when she was pregnant. We were making plans."

"Do you remember what clothes she was wearing the last time you saw her?"

"Just that it was one of those long dresses they make the women wear. She had a light brown sweater too."

"Good. Zander, Give me a general description of her. Height, weight, hair colour," Jess scribbled furiously at notes. "Do you know where her family lives?"

"She left home because of them. I only know she said Vancouver."

"Do you happen to know her birthday?"

"October eighth. She was eighteen then."

"Why didn't you come to the detachment when this happened?" Her tone was sharper than she intended.

Zander looked stricken. "Something in me wondered if she really had just left, you know? Maybe she didn't love me and was confused because of the pregnancy. I shouldn't have thought like that but… anyway, time passed and I decided she was just gone."

"Okay, Zander. You need to come into the detachment and make a report. Give a description of her, lock down some dates. Can we count on you to do that?"

"Yeah, I'll do it for Mariah."

"Good. Here's my contact numbers if there's anything more you want to tell me. Okay?"

"Okay. Thanks for listening."

"Be sure to come in and file a report."

Zander nodded, hooked his arm through Carl's and made soothing noises to the agitated man as they walked away.

Jess and Todd walked up to the porch of the Goodwin house. It looked old enough to be part of an original settlement almost a century ago. The house had obviously been renovated with new siding and roof. But the windows looked old with a stained glass transom over the front door. The stairs were in good repair but the grey paint was peeling. They knocked and the door was quickly opened.

"We saw you coming," Charlotte said. "Come in. Joy's putting some coffee on."

She led them to the kitchen, a small room in an earlier style, plain wooden cabinets and linoleum floors. "I can't help but comment on your name," Jess said. "Is Charlotte after the town?"

"My great-grandfather settled the town a hundred years ago and named it after my great-grandmother. So," she finished, "we know most people in town, past and present."

Charlotte's sister, Joy Baines, poured coffee all around without asking who wanted it. She was used to playing hostess to the close-knit community that was Charlotte Ridge.

"I guess you're here because of the body," Charlotte said bluntly as she eased her bulk into a chair.

"I'm sure this has put everyone on edge," Jess started. "We are hoping that talking about it will jog some memories and give us a line of inquiry." She related to the sisters what forensics had discovered so far. "Does that describe anyone, bring anything to mind?"

Charlotte and Joy looked at each other and Joy gave a questioning look to her sister.

"We've talked about this," Charlotte said. "People come and go through Charlotte Ridge, especially through the summer. It could be anybody. We have three cabins we rent out. They're all strangers until they start coming back year after year for hunting and fishing." She looked at her sister again. "But, we wonder about a doctor who went missing from Cranbrook about three years ago, wasn't it, Joy? Were you guys here, then?" she asked the constables.

"Yes, we both were," Todd finally said. He was quiet today. Had been since they left the office, Jess noticed. But then, she had been too.

"Well, her name was Aimée-Marie Chandler. You probably remember that she disappeared. Everyone knew about it. There was a lot of publicity in trying to find her. You'll find her in your missing persons' files."

"Yes, I remember it," Jess said. Todd nodded too.

"In the end, her husband was in the bullseye for it but the public was told there was no real suspect, only a person of interest. That's what was made public, anyway. We only suspected it was the husband, as many domestic situations go. But, a lot of us knew the husband through his work and nobody could see him harming her. But, they always say that, don't they, the friends and neighbours, that it was such a shock and so on." With that, Charlotte seemed to run out of steam. Todd took notes.

"Was anything in particular happening in the area at that time? Did anyone to your knowledge remark about strange people or events?"

"Well, it was a long time ago to remember strange cars or anything. There is always a summer music festival which brings strangers to town. So it could be a stranger in that grave, someone passing through. I doubt you'll get very far with that." Charlotte continued to speak for them and Joy remained silent. Once, Jess thought Joy was about to say something but pulled back in deference to her sister.

"Do you remember any altercations or feuds going on that everyone was talking about, things known to the community?"

"Oh, there are frequently squabbles. Families can be cantankerous, can't they?"

"Is there any family in particular?" Todd was scribbling, filling the page.

"Can't say I want to highlight anyone. If I think on it some more I can get back to you." Charlotte drained her mug and stood. "Good luck to you on this. Charlotte Ridge is generally a quiet little place. Maybe this will shake free some memories."

Jess and Todd took last swallows of their coffee and stood. "Thanks for your time," Jess said at the door. She handed Charlotte a card. "Just in case something comes to mind."

They walked towards the Heath house. "I think the Goodwin sisters are good people to know," Jess said.

"Agreed. There's nothing like a local historian," Todd answered.

They approached the grey vinyl house and Michael Heath quickly opened his door to their knock. "Come in. My wife, Eva, is here too." The house was small and crowded with books and newspapers. It was apparent that the couple loved to collect to the point of compulsion. Piles of books and papers filled the living room and hallway. It made maneuvering in the house difficult. A computer sat on a table facing a window to the main road through town. The dog, Mack, had stood tail wagging as they entered but quickly retreated to napping under the computer desk.

The officers weren't invited to sit and Todd took out his notebook.

"So, Mr. Heath, what can you tell me about finding the skeleton?"

Heath made his statement which Todd read back to him. It varied little from the information he gave at the burial site the morning of the discovery.

"We'll get it typed up. Come in to the office to sign it the next time you're in Cranbrook."

"Sure. Thanks for coming to me. Saves me a trip to the city,"

Jess and Todd walked back towards the General Store where their car was parked. Coming out of the store was a big man, long hair with beard. Jess was pleasantly startled to recognize Dr. Bruce carrying groceries.

"Hey," she said, "my hero." She reached out and touched his arm, smiling all the while.

Todd, tense by her side, digested the word hero, saw the casual touch which set up an immediate dislike for the man in front of him. The man smiled down at Jess, a happy grin spreading across his face.

"Todd, this is Dr. Bruce who rescued me. Are you finished your shopping? Could we drive you back up the road? It's the least we can do after you rescued me so well."

"This is unexpected and so welcome. I'll accept a ride if you're sure. No more business in town?"

"We're just asking people about the body that was found. Surely, you heard about it."

"Flo just mentioned it. Disturbing to say the least." Jess opened the back door of the car for him.

They all settled into seats, Jess and Todd in front, Todd driving. He asked Jess which direction to go and pulled out.

"I don't suppose you can add to the information. Your life is pretty isolated."

"I'll admit the news I get is late in the day, or week for that matter, but, no, I don't know anything about the body."

They quickly reached the spot in the road where Dr. Bruce got out. To Todd's surprise, Jess got out of the car and said goodbye softly and squeezed his hand as he held hers in both of his. He left and disappeared into the bush. Todd took it all in with dismay bordering on shock. Jess was acting as if that man was important to her, emotionally important, that they were close somehow. With the looks on their faces the touch was practically foreplay. His lips compressed into a tight line and he seethed as they drove away.

The encounter had given Jess an inner jolt of happiness. She hugged it to her on the drive back to Cranbrook. By the time they reached the detachment she had reviewed everything she and Dr. Bruce had ever said to each other, had it encapsulated in a little bubble to be brought out and examined whenever she wanted.

Back at the barn, Todd kept Jess in his line of vision. He could tell her mind wasn't on her work, too much staring into space, small, silent smiles. Who was that hairy hermit anyway? How could Jess, or anyone for that matter, develop such obvious closeness with a man who looks like a gorilla and lives a survival lifestyle in the bush? He would check outstanding warrants to see if any fit the man. Pinning something on his sorry ass would be a pleasure.

Walking the path back to his cabin and thinking about the newly discovered body, Dr. Adam Chandler felt the stirring of unease. When he'd stood in the General Store and the gossip about the body swirled around him, he'd taken a minute to collect himself. The whole notion of an unknown body had shaken him and twisted his insides. Several minutes passed before he calmed himself. A body had been found, a skeletonized body which meant it could be any age. The notion that it was some old settler from British Columbia's early days fit. He hoped it turned out that way.

The mystery of his wife's disappearance had never been solved and could attract renewed interest any time. He bet that time was now. He knew authorities would need some forensic data to proceed with identification. Part of him welcomed it. Part of him didn't want that circus to start up again. He didn't want the police sifting through his life and marriage, didn't want the court of public opinion to convict him again. It was all too heavy. His solitary life now was peaceful; he had everything he needed as long as his funds held out. Money from his house sale and investments went a long way when you lived in the bush.

Then Jessica Morell was at his shoulder, speaking his name. He startled at her in the disconcerting uniform. The face, the lovely face was still there. But, the authority that went with the uniform intruded. He had recognized her when she stayed at his cabin but kept that to himself. He remembered her as the cop that had heart. She hadn't judged him. Then, Jess was talking and he smiled as best he could, heard her introduce him to her partner and then he was accepting a ride home.

As he'd said goodbye and started his trek home through the bush, he hoped he had pulled off the same casual attitude he had at the cabin, that nothing had changed in his demeanor towards her. But his feelings had changed. He and Jess had been living a fantasy, playing a game that was role-play. Cocooned in the cabin they played their parts, each another person swept into a fairy tale of a cabin in the woods and the gentle giant of a woodsman who saved the lost damsel. Things would change between them now that their real roles became clear. He still hoped that she would come back to visit but, history was stirring, ready to raise its disquieting head and look directly at him.

CHAPTER 15

A REVIEW OF THE MISSING PERSONS' files brought up four possible identities. Two female cousins in their early twenties had disappeared two years ago. When the family was contacted they said that the girls had been reported in Vancouver and neither girl owned a black leather coat. There was also the recent filing by Zander Nilsson. His friend Mariah Talman, also known as Charity, had disappeared about three years ago. Henley was searching social media for any reference to her, so far without luck. She hadn't been reported missing by any family members. There were no birth records of an infant born to Mariah Talman. She had simply slipped off the radar.

The fourth identity was Aimée-Marie Chandler. The gender, age and time missing fit. Notes from her missing report described a black leather coat that was gone from her home and that she was probably wearing the night she went to the hospital.

Dr. Adam Chandler had left town six months after his wife's disappearance so was no longer available to help identify the coat fragments. Tooth pulp extracted from the skeleton for a DNA profile was a match to Aimée-Marie Chandler.

"We have to find the doctor. He was our number one suspect when she disappeared and, even though it appears a vehicle hit, remains a suspect until we can rule him out." Sturgis assigned Corporal Thayer to find him. "Check property tax rolls; check with BCMA to see if he is practicing anywhere. If not try the CMA. Credit cards, phone records, driver's license, Facebook. Do it all.

"Morell, check to see if she has other family, parents, siblings. They need to be notified before we go public with this. They might know where Dr. Adam is."

"Yes, sir," Jess said. "I remember three years ago that Aimée Chandler's parents came out for a few weeks when she went missing. They were from Ontario. I'll try her friends, see if they can help."

"Good. All the interviews from three years ago have to be done again," Sturgis said. The room groaned. "This time we know what happened to her. It gives us leverage. It might also give us motive. Think about money, sex, revenge when you talk to people."

"Staff Sergeant, do you really see the husband as a suspect if it's a vehicle hit at three a.m.?" Jess asked.

"Yeah, I know. It puts him farther down the list. But people are most often killed by family and friends and we can't afford to overlook him. After all, this body was buried. Not your typical hit and run. And we only have his word for it that she didn't make it home. There are various ways it could have played out so the good doc's still on the list."

"Got it."

Aimée-Marie Chandler. Dr. Adam. Dr. Adam with long hair and beard. It danced around in her brain for a minute, but no longer. Then, an overwhelming realization jolted her. It spread through her the way a tsunami overtakes the shore, unstoppable and rushing at her, swamping her. She couldn't breathe. She recalled her interviews with Dr. Adam three years ago, the way he ran his hand through his hair, the slight slant to his eyes, the rich brown of his hair. Could Dr. Bruce be Dr. Adam? He was leaner, as to be expected living the way he does, less soft and more muscular. The beard and long hair obscured the better part of his face, but, the basics were there. Dr. Adam had left town some months after his wife disappeared. Did he find solace in the isolation of the bush? Or was he running from what he had done?

Appearances couldn't be trusted. Her budding feelings for him especially couldn't be trusted. She had even been considering his invitation to spend the night, again. Now, there was a sense of betrayal and she didn't even know what was true, what false. She needed to find out who he was, what he did or didn't do. He'd said he would tell her his name on the next visit. Would he be truthful, especially if he was hiding from the law? Not likely. So if he actually admitted to being Dr. Adam, does that give him a pass as the killer?

Nobody gets a pass. She had to find out. She decided to go to see him now while the sun was still high. She'd talk to Aimée-Marie's friends later.

She looked over at Thayer working away online to try to find Adam Chandler. She knew she was derelict, guilty of obstruction, if she didn't tell him what she knew… but, she felt a need to confront the doctor on her own. She could do that much. She thought she owed him.

During the drive to Charlotte Ridge Jess thought out how to talk to Adam Chandler, what to say and how to say it. He wouldn't know yet that the body is that of his wife. She would deliver the news that would possibly be a shock but should also bring relief, that is, if he is innocent of any violence to her. If he killed her she had to be prepared for anything. She was taking a chance going solo. She knew that protocol and safety said she should have a partner with her. She considered his gentle nature. She'd chance it.

She stopped at the two rocks that marked the path into the woods. The path was becoming familiar and she was soon at the cabin. She found him at the garden putting in stakes for green beans using a hatchet head as a hammer. Shirt off, his back glistened with sweat. He looked up.

She stood in place as they looked at each other across the yard. She was in uniform. This was official.

He opened his mouth to say something, swallowed then said, "You know."

She nodded.

"It's her isn't it?" A jumble of emotions played across his face, his distress obvious.

"Yes."

He put aside the stake he was holding and set the hatchet on a stump.

"Adam, I…,"

"How did it happen? Can they tell?"

"Yes. She was hit by a vehicle at high speed. She had many injuries and would have died quickly." His face twisted with pain, grief. Tears were on the surface. He gulped a breath, his knees jackknifed and he slumped to the ground. His hands shook as he swiped at his eyes. Jess took a step towards him wishing to comfort, then, stopped herself.

"Adam, my boss is trying to find you," she said in a choked voice.

"You didn't tell them about me?"

"No, not yet. I owe you too much. But, you need to come in, to talk."

He looked up at her. "You were there that night, weren't you? The night it happened. I remember you."

"It took me till today to put it together." It took everything in her to stay rooted to her spot and not go to him.

"Can it wait until tomorrow? I need to clean up a bit." He indicated his beard and hair and looked up at her.

She considered waiting as an option and knew that was problematic. He had money, probably a passport. He was a flight risk. But, he'd had three years to disappear and he hadn't done it. Her job was on the line.

"I'll trust that you come in tomorrow, no later. Can you tell me if she had parents or siblings to notify?"

"Her parents, Meena and Kelly Carlisle in Lindsay, Ontario. I think they're still alive, but I haven't talked to them in a long time." He got up off the ground. "Thank you for being the one to tell me. I couldn't have handled it if I heard through the General Store gossip."

"As I said, I owe you."

"There is no debt. Will I see you tomorrow?"

"Probably. I'm in and out of the office."

"I won't say you sent me in. I'll blame that on the grapevine."

"Thank you." She stood awkwardly for a moment then turned and walked away, so many things left unsaid.

The media announcement naming Aimée-Marie Chandler as the unknown body appeared on the evening news. Watching from her house in Charlotte Ridge, Joy Baines sucked back air and shook her head in dismay. It had taken too long to come to this. It should have been finished three years ago.

While Charlotte cooked in the kitchen, she picked up the phone and dialed the RCMP detachment. "I have information about Aimée-Marie Chandler," she told the switchboard. She was put through to homicide and talked to Corporal Abel Thayer who was fielding calls. The phone had started ringing as soon as the broadcast ended, tips that would go nowhere and eat up man hours.

"Who's speaking, please?" Thayer said.

"I'm Joy Baines. I made a statement about the doctor when she went missing. I still think it's important and I want to talk to someone."

"What can you tell me, Ms. Baines?"

Joy Baines took a breath. "I wonder if she was having an affair."

"Why do you say that?"

"Because I saw her one day in Kimberly. I was at an office building, a medical clinic, next to a hotel and she came out of the hotel with a small suitcase and a man with his arm over her shoulders. They kissed, on the lips, before they parted on the street. They went different directions."

"Did you recognize the man?" Thayer sat up straighter.

"He's local, to Cranbrook, I mean. His face is familiar but, it definitely wasn't her husband. I don't know his name."

"Describe him." Joy did her best but time had blurred the memory. "Can you come in to the station and talk to us about this?"

"Tomorrow? Sure. I have to say I did report this before, like when she went missing and nobody called me."

"I'll check through our file. Give me your phone number, Ms. Baines."

Thayer took details and rang off stressing to the caller that it was important that she come in and make a statement. He figured they'd finally caught a break. This was one of the best motives possible for the husband to kill her. It confirmed what had been said when she disappeared. Excited, he took it to the Staff Sergeant.

Cathy Aikens was putting dinner on the table as the evening news revealed that Aimée-Marie Chandler's body had been found. The casserole wobbled in her hands as she lowered it to the table. Kevin Aikens stared transfixed at the television, stomach lurching as the details emerged.

As long as Aimée remained missing their life would continue without disturbance. Things between them were stable if not perfect. Whose marriage was perfect? The kids were the barometer of the family's health and the kids were happy and progressing well at school.

This news could shatter everything they'd worked at for the last few years. All the work they had put into their renewed relationship would be put to the test. Aimée was to blame. Aimée had ruined everything and now she was coming back to do it again.

CHAPTER 16

"WE HAVE A MOTIVE, PEOPLE," Sturgis told the squad room. He related the information taken from a phone call, a witness to Aimée-Marie Chandler's movements. "It was a year before she disappeared but that really doesn't matter. The possibility of an affair has come up again and maybe her husband knew about it. It's not the doctor in Kelowna that we already know about. We need more information." The tips' line had had a flurry of activity after the media release but had slowed now. Just the one solid lead.

"Morell, go back to her friends, Dr. Kinsey and Cathy Aikens. Press for info about an affair, sexual indiscretion, whatever. If anyone knows it's girlfriends. Go with Henley but you take the lead. She may talk more freely to a woman.

"Thayer, how's that search going? We need Chandler."

Jess's stomach quivered. She was holding back

information on a police investigation. Obstructing it. She could be charged. Adam had to come through as he said and come to the detachment on his own today. She was putting a lot of faith in someone she didn't know very well.

"Let's go," Henley said. "I've signed out a car." He was ready to go. Jess put on her jacket and cap and followed him to the car park. "You have the addresses?"

"Yeah." She indicated the direction and Todd started out.

They drove across the city, Jess into her thoughts, Todd into his. She couldn't get her mind off her visit to Adam yesterday. They were both so restrained, their lighthearted relationship suddenly turned serious. Todd couldn't stop thinking about Jess and the other man, a big hairy man who held her hand and softened when he looked at her. He didn't like it, didn't like it at all.

"Jess, I'm...,"

"We're here," she said and jumped out of the car. She didn't like the way Todd had been looking at her lately. His eyes followed her around the squad room. Hungry eyes. He looked at her with hungry eyes ready to devour her. True they hadn't had sex in quite a long time, longer than they had ever gone. But, she didn't like the possessiveness of the look, almost like he was claiming her. Her feelings about Todd were changing. He didn't hold the attraction that he once had. Was her relationship with Todd over? Was there another night of intimacy between them? She had to decide what to do about Todd.

Inside the medical building, the receptionist buzzed Megan Kinsey telling her that police wanted to talk to her.

"You're back." Megan Kinsey's greeting was abrupt bordering on rude.

"Well, it has been three years, doctor. And, since we've found the body of your friend, I would think you'd be a bit more interested, if not curious and distraught."

Kinsey seemed to deflate. She sat heavily onto the chair behind the desk. Jess noted the picture of a child on the shelf behind the desk and figured it was the one she was pregnant with on their earlier interview.

"I'm sorry," the doctor said. "My emotions are all over the place since I heard the news. I really hoped she had left town on her own." At this point her eyes moistened and she swallowed back emotion.

"What makes you think she might do that, stay away this long without contacting her husband?"

Kinsey looked stricken and said nothing. Jess prodded. "Was there another man in her life? Was she involved with someone she might have left with?"

Kinsey opened her mouth slightly, held back what she was about to say.

"Doctor? This is quite likely a murder inquiry. If you can provide information it's your duty to do so."

"I, uh, yeah, think she was seeing someone."

"Did she talk about it? Tell you any details?"

"Just once. She had just come back from one of her out-of-town excursions and I asked her how the retreat was." She stopped.

"And?"

"She said retreats are always better if there's someone to share it with. She had a dreamy smile on her face when she said it."

"Did you ask who he was?"

"No. I wasn't going to pry. If she wanted me to know she would have told me. I was waiting for her to be ready."

"And she never told you?"

"No."

"Any clues, ever, as to who he might be? Did she mention anything descriptive? Height, weight? Any comments about his job?"

"The only thing she said was that it was better to share a retreat experience, 'But that's sometimes difficult to arrange,' was her comment"

"Which means he's married or otherwise involved."

Kinsey shrugged. "I guess," she said. She suddenly looked worried. "Please don't destroy her in public. She was a good person and Adam a good husband."

"Her actions speak for themselves, Doctor. We only follow where the leads take us. Why didn't you tell us this three years ago? It might have helped us find her."

"I thought she had a right to her private life. I didn't see any harm in it."

"Really, Dr. Kinsey? You can't be that naïve." She turned to Henley, who had been standing silently behind her, and who went out the door first. They left.

"That really didn't tell us much more than we knew from the witness," Henley said.

"No, but corroboration of a witness statement is always good. It's just three years too late."

She referred to notes for Cathy Aikens' address. "Let's see what her other friend has to say." The Aikens still lived at the same place, the two story stucco in the family neighbourhood. They rang the doorbell repeatedly with no answer until they were walking away and Cathy Aikens appeared at the door. She was tousled and sleepy and wore a housecoat over pajamas.

"Oh. I was sleeping. I worked nights last night." She indicated the officers follow her inside.

"I'm sorry, Mrs. Aikens. I should have thought about shift work."

"It's okay. I'm not going in tonight so I needed only a short sleep to switch over." She yawned and cleared her throat. "Coffee? I could use it."

"If you're making it," Jess said.

She filled a carafe with water and put it into the drip machine. "I'm not surprised you're here. To finally know what happened is a relief."

"Relief? We don't know much. We still don't know how her body got where it did. Who put it there? That doesn't sound like relief to me."

"I mean," Aikens said somewhat flustered, "we can at least put her to rest properly, say our goodbyes."

"There is that," Jess said. "Cathy, we have a witness who saw Aimée-Marie in a compromising situation with a man. We are following the likelihood that she was having an affair. What can you tell me about that?"

Cathy's back was to them as she got mugs out of the cupboard. Jess didn't miss the hesitation in her reach.

"You know something about it, don't you?"

"I don't know what you mean. Aimée would never cheat on Adam." She didn't lie well. Her neck and face broke out in red blotches. She tried to sound casual but the truth was written all over her face.

"Cathy, this is an unnatural death investigation, possibly a murder. You have to tell me what you know. It's vitally important. That man, whoever he is, could have killed her."

"I don't think you're on the right track. Nobody who knew Aimée would ever kill her." Now her hand trembled as she put sugar in her coffee.

"I can see where this shakes you up and you have a right to be upset. Nobody deserves to die this way."

"I don't know anything to help you. Aimée was my friend and I want to help catch whoever did this, but I can't. I thought she'd just gone away for a break."

"And didn't ever come back? A bit strange, don't you think?"

"Aimée was… unpredictable."

"Really? Unpredictable? She was a doctor with responsibilities who according to her husband wouldn't just disappear." Jess skewered Cathy with hard eyes. "You're whole demeanor tells me there is something you are hiding. You know something that we should know."

Cathy collapsed, hands wrapped around her face and started crying. "I don't know anything, I swear." She snuffled and reached for a tea towel to wipe her face.

"It must involve someone you know or you wouldn't be this distraught. This is Aimée's life and death we're talking about. Her death, Cathy."

Cathy sat up stiffening her spine. "You can't badger me like this. I don't have to take it."

"We'll see. Get dressed. We'll continue this at the detachment."

Cathy's mouth fell open in shock. She compressed her lips and rose from the chair. When she left the kitchen Jess said, "She's lying. She knows something."

"If she really wanted to help she'd tell us," Henley said. "Why wouldn't she want that?"

"Because she's protecting someone. Maybe just the man Aimée was with, maybe a murderer. If she feels she has to protect someone, then, it's someone who means something to her. Or she's involved herself. Why else block the investigation? I'll bet Sturgis would want her in the barn for an intense interview. We'll see what she says then."

❧

The Nilsson General Store buzzed with shoppers and the coffee crowd. Auggie Rymes lounged in a chair tilted back. His son, Keith, hovered over his shoulder.

"So who's watching the garage?" someone asked. "Or don't you have any business these days?" It was a friendly taunt that Auggie shrugged off.

"If anyone needs me they know where to find me," he said dismissively. "I am wanted by some people, you know," he added suggestively.

The group guffawed and one person threw a spit ball at him. "In your dreams," the man said.

Carl Thurlow wandered into the store, his cowboy hat pulled down low over his eyes. He found Flo who opened a soda for him and sat him beside the counter. The group eyed Carl, some more interested than others. "Is he still fixated on that body?" Michael Heath said. "Every time I see him he's muttering about digging a hole."

"We all saw the hole," someone said.

"He's just crazy, old Carl is. Things get stuck in his head and can't find a way out."

Carl sat in his place, rocking slightly, sipping his drink as Brother Jedidiah in robes topped by a ski sweater came to the counter and asked questions of Flo. She began gathering grocery goods for him. Carl looked up at the tall man.

"You dug a hole, a hole for sin," he said.

Brother Jedidiah frowned at the strange man in the cowboy hat. "I dig lots of holes," he said then turned away from Carl.

"Leave the man alone, Carl," Flo said. "He's plants a big garden like lots of other people."

"You dug a hole for sin," Carl repeated. "Yep, yep, you buried a sin." He bobbed his head up and down.

Brother Jedidiah turned red and clamped both mouth and fists. Sweat appeared on his face.

Seeing the Brother's discomfort Flo said, "Don't mind him. He's often confused."

The robed man looked up from Carl to Flo. He was

breathing heavily but took in her words and relaxed his stance. He nodded his head, paid for his groceries and left giving Carl a backward look as he did. He stared at Carl, then, walked on.

Flo soothed Carl as he finished his drink and said, "That man, that man. Don't like that man. Going home, home to Bobby."

"Sure, sure. Good, Carl. Good idea."

Carl had made very clear statements that Michael Heath heard amidst the chatter of the group. Heath's attention had focused on Carl and Brother Jedidiah. Heath had seen the Brother many times while walking on the ridge and was disturbed by the intensity of the man. Carl could be equally intense but people usually paid no attention to his rambling. Heath did.

Brother Jedidiah dug a hole for sin. Carl clearly had something in mind when he said that. *You buried a sin*, Carl had said. With a newly discovered buried body on his mind it made a person think.

Carl got up and left through the back door walking along the access road behind the row of stores and restaurants. He shuffled as he walked, stirring up dust and kicking pebbles along the way. His emotions had eased since leaving the store and was startled when the robed man drove up beside him and stopped. Carl stopped too at the side of the road and stared as the man got out of the van. His body tensed as the man approached him.

"You," he said pointing an angry finger at Carl,

"Stop talking about digging a hole, do you hear me?" Brother Jedidiah ground out. "Do you understand me?"

Carl took a step back, frightened and shook his head. "You dug a big hole and sin went in."

Jedidiah stepped forward and grabbed Carl around the neck. He pressed hard on his throat. "I said, stop talking. Stop talking!" he shouted. His fist came back and punched Carl in the side of the head. Carl lost his footing and fell to the ground. The fist came down again and cracked his nose causing blood to spray across his face and chest. Carl cried out, moaned and collapsed unmoving. The assailant grabbed him by the clothes and brought Carl's face up close.

"Don't say another word about digging holes or I'll come back and kill you. Got that? You've never seen me before. You don't know me, got that?"

Carl didn't respond. His eyes were closed and breathing noisy, clogged as he was with blood in nose and throat. Brother Jedidiah shoved him back onto the ground, got into the van and drove off leaving Carl swimming in and out of consciousness by the side of the road.

Michael Heath coming out of the back door of the store saw the van drive away from a crumpled heap in the ground. He picked up speed, running down the road, and was soon staring down at a bloodied Carl Thurlow. He got out his cell phone and called for help.

CHAPTER 17

"WE'VE BROUGHT YOU IN HERE because we think you can be more help than you've been so far." Staff Sergeant Sturgis dropped a notepad on the table between him and Cathy Aikens. She jumped at the noise and, Jess across from her, could see the woman was wound pretty tight.

Cathy's eyes darted between the two officers. "I've told you all I know." Her hands moved nervously in her lap. Her mismatched clothes said that she was frantic and distracted when she dressed.

"We don't think you have. We think you are holding something back. You see, we've been in this business for quite a while and read people well. You're obviously not as forthcoming as you've presented. Now," he leaned across the desk, "we want whatever it is you haven't said, whatever information you have about Aimée-Marie that might help us find her killer. You're protecting someone, aren't you?"

Cathy's lips quivered and her eyes became moist. She swallowed.

"We'll sit here as long as it takes." Sturgis was determined.

Jess felt sorry for her. There was that soft heart again. Cathy had been at work at the time of Aimée's disappearance so she wasn't personally involved. Maybe. Probably. There was always the chance that she conspired with someone. It was the innocent bystanders that got to her. Collateral damage, so to speak.

"What do you know?" Jess asked. "You're upset about something." She used a soothing voice in contrast to Sturgis and hoped for the response they were after.

Cathy swallowed again. "My husband. He had an affair with Aimée." She crumbled into tears laying her head in her arms on the table.

"When was this?" Jess asked.

Cathy raised her head. "About four years ago."

"So it was long over when she disappeared?"

"So they said." Cathy gulped, wiped tears from her face.

"But you weren't sure." It was a statement.

"How can a wife ever be sure about that?" She'd lowered her eyes in embarrassment at being betrayed.

"So you knew about it and continued to be friends with Aimée?"

Cathy shrugged. "Kevin and Aimée were remorseful. Each swore it was a one-off. Kevin and I had been having some problems around then. It was an impulsive mistake and we all knew it."

"Dr. Adam knew it too?"

"Yes. But he's never spoken of it to me. He thinks I don't know."

"So that leaves just about everyone with a motive to kill Aimée-Marie Chandler," Sturgis stated.

"Not Kevin. Since we all knew about it there was no motive for him. And I would never hurt Aimée. Yes, I was devastated when this happened but we got over it, all of us."

"So you say." He waited a beat. "We know where you were the night Aimée went missing. Where was your husband?"

Shock spread across Cathy's face. "Why home with the children. I was working nights."

"And he couldn't have left the house during the night?"

"No, of course not. He wouldn't leave the kids." Cathy had recovered some starch in her demeanor and looked Sturgis in the eye. "Nobody would hurt Aimée."

"Somebody did." Sturgis stood. "See her out will you, Morell." Cathy left and Sturgis stood thoughtfully. "Tell Franks to go and pick up Kevin Aikens. We need a formal talk. We don't really know that the affair was over, do we, or that he stayed home that night? Not on a wife's say-so we don't."

Colleen put a call through to Jess at her desk. "It's the hospital. They've got an assault victim and the man who found him wants to talk to you."

"Get his name and tell him to wait there. I'm on my way."

Jess grabbed her jacket, told Thayer where she was going and quickly reached the hospital. A cacophony of the usual emergency room noises hit Jess as the automatic doors opened in front of her. Staff directed her to Carl Thurlow and she found him semi-conscious on a gurney with Michael Heath at his side. Heath was drinking an energy drink from a can. Carl's eyes were blinking and once in a while he called for Flo. Even through the blood and bruises Jess recognized him as the challenged man who had been with Zander Nilsson. Wasn't he talking about digging a hole then?

"Mr. Heath," Jess said as she offered her hand. "You're on the spot, again. You saw this?"

"Sort of. I saw Carl lying on the side of the road as a van drove away. I know who was driving the van but I didn't see him hit Carl."

"Who?"

"That Brother Jedidiah from the commune. Carl had been in the store when Jedidiah came in. Carl accused him of digging a hole to bury a body. To bury sin. All of us at the store heard it. Then Carl left and I guess that Jed guy followed him and beat him up."

"Any idea what Carl was talking about?"

"Only as much as the next person. Maybe that body that was found a few days ago. Makes sense. Carl is often up on the ridge, sleeps up there too." He gave Carl a glance with pity in his eyes.

She turned to Carl and called his name. Carl looked

at her with blackened eyes. "Carl? My name's Jessica. I'm a police officer. I want to find who did this. Can you tell me? Who beat you up, Carl?"

"Got out of the car and beat me. That's a sin he did." Now there were tears in the corner of his eyes.

"Yes, it was a sin. Did you know him? Who was it Carl?"

"He wore a dress like Jesus. He shouldn't sin." The words from cut and swollen lips were difficult to catch. "Beard, tall."

There was more than one tall man at the commune dressed in robes with a beard. Jess turned to Heath. "You didn't happen to see any of the license plate, did you?"

"I didn't. But if you want me to I can drive up there and look."

"No, I'll do it. Thank you for your help with this." She turned back to Carl. "I'll find out who did this, don't worry." As she was leaving she spoke to the doctor about Carl's injuries and was told there were no bones broken. He should recover fully.

Then, Flo Nilsson hurried into the ER, worry on her face. She stopped when she saw Jess and the doctor. "How is he? Who did this?"

"I'm going to find a picture to show him," Jess said. "Hopefully he can identify him."

"Good. Good. Oh, the poor thing," she said as she hurried to Carl's bedside to console the young man and relieve Michael Heath.

"Thanks, Doctor. If you could send a report to the detachment that would be great." Heath walked out with Jess and stopped at his SUV. He pulled a pack of cigarettes from his jacket and lit up dragging the smoke deeply into his lungs.

"Poor bastard," he said pityingly. "Imagine taking advantage of someone like that."

"The world isn't kind, Mr. Heath. We all know that." She left Heath at his car and headed back to the barn.

Adam Chandler walked into the police detachment and identified himself. He asked to speak to the person in charge of the investigation into the death of Aimée-Marie Chandler. Colleen buzzed Sturgis and showed Dr. Adam to the Staff Sergeant's office.

Sturgis stood as Chandler walked into his office. He could see the former suspect in the man in front of him but the change was remarkable. Chandler, now toned, muscular and twenty pounds thinner, was an imposing figure. His beard had been trimmed to a neat one inch and hair cut to just over his ears. His tanned face had a determined set to it and Sturgis could see he wasn't to be intimidated.

"So it's really my wife's body?"

"Confirmed by DNA. I'm sorry. Please, sit down."

"Have you found anything?"

"We have some artifacts from the burial site. I want to ask you about them. Stay here. I'll get them" Sturgis left the room to retrieve the evidence bags from the Exhibit Vault. He signed for them and returned to the office to find Chandler standing behind the chair. Sturgis placed the bags in a row in front of Adam.

"This is a piece of a leather coat with a metal button. Do you recognize it?"

Adam's throat closed for a moment but he swallowed passed it and said, "That's Aimée's coat. Yes, I recognize it."

Sturgis pushed the glove towards him. "What about this?"

"It looks like any canvas work glove. I don't recognize it."

"It was in the burial site. We assume that whoever put her there dropped it. We hope to get some DNA from it. Any chance we'll find yours there?"

"Are you still playing this game, Sturgis? No, it's not a glove from my place. I know nothing more than I did three years ago. It looks like you folks don't either."

"We have made some progress investigating possibilities." He pushed the final evidence bag a few inches. "Do you smoke, doctor?"

"No. Never have. That's a lot of cigarette butts. Where did they come from?"

"Someone goes to the site and stands there and smokes. Maybe someone who knows something. If we can match DNA from the glove to the cigarettes we're a step closer to solving this."

"And if you can't…?'

"We keep working." Sturgis shuffled some papers. "It's been three years and you've had time to think about things. Is there anything that you can tell us now that has come to mind over time?"

"You haven't found her car?"

"No."

"Kevin Aikens and I looked for it along the route she would have taken home from the hospital. The area is forested and dense, deep cliffs and sidehills. We didn't find a thing."

"Actually, we did the same thing. No luck. The car has disappeared. Now that we know she ended up on the ridge, we've been looking there but no luck."

Adam stood. "I'm staying at the Days Inn for a few days. When do you think they'll release the body? There are funeral arrangements to make."

"We notified her parents. I'll get back to you. Do you have a cell phone number?"

"You notified Meena and Kelly? I can't imagine how hard this must be… but, I'm feeling some of it myself so I guess I can." He paused a thoughtful moment. "I don't have a cell phone. I haven't kept up with that." He walked out of the room. Jess was standing in the hallway and stopped short when she saw him.

"You made it," she said.

"Was there any doubt?" he said quietly and gave a half-hearted grin.

"No. I knew you'd come through." His new look was good on him. The sport shirt and khakis were new.

They chatted briefly. He told her where he was staying. He invited her for dinner.

"Uh, I have to decline. You're part of an investigation.

I'm afraid I have to draw some lines. I'm sorry. Truly," she said softly.

He reached for her hand and she pulled back breaking contact. "After this is over, then…"

"Yes, then we'll see. I know where to find you. You know where to find me."

Across the room Todd Henley looked on watching the police officer and the suspect engage in a much too friendly way. He didn't like what he saw. In fact, as he watched the scene unfold, anger gripped him. He could practically see the arc of electricity between them when their hands met. His whole body tightened and an overwhelming rage swept through him. Chandler had no right! No right to a girl like Jess. Jess was his and only his. Chandler was still their best suspect, probably a killer. Maybe he thought playing up to Jess would loosen the tightrope the RCMP had on him. Oh, he was smart. But Todd was smarter. Chandler wasn't going to get away with it.

Todd followed Adam out of the building. He felt his mission settle on him like a coat of armour, tough and defensible. It was up to him to save Jess from Adam Chandler. Save her from herself, for him. He had to see where the killer was staying.

CHAPTER 18

Jess told Sturgis she was going to get the license plate number of Brother Jedidiah's van. It was time they knew his real name. She said that Carl Thurlow had described him in the assault but couldn't name him. They needed a picture from his driver's license.

"Okay," Sturgis said, "but take Franks with you. You shouldn't go there alone. Just look at the vehicle and come back."

Jess signaled to Franks that they needed to go. He was on the phone in an intense conversation with someone. She waited. Franks' head was bent over the phone, obviously something important. Jess became restless. They needed to know who brother Jedidiah was. She shifted foot to foot. "C'mon, Joe, c'mon." She peered at him, willing him to feel her frustration. Finally, she couldn't take any more waiting and left.

The drive to Charlotte Ridge was short and enjoyable as she knew it would be with afternoon sun warming the squad car. After all, this was an easy assignment and they would soon know who beat Carl Thurlow. She made the turn at Ridge Road and was quickly at the commune compound. The Brother's van was in the drive. No one was in sight. She brought the car to a stop and got out, took out her note pad and copied the plate number.

"What do you think you're doing?" The voice was behind her. She turned and found Brother Jedidiah closing in on her. Long hair hanging in dank strands, his face was contorted with anger.

"Just what you see, sir. Your legal name is of interest to us. Or you could keep it simple and just tell me."

"You're on private property. I don't want intrusion by anyone and that's my right."

"As long as you don't intrude in others' lives."

Brother Jedidiah knew at once that he was in trouble. He advanced on her. Jess could see a clear intention in his movement to overpower her. She reached for her sidearm but the tall man grabbed her arm with one hand and swung her into a headlock with the other. He was choking her with both arms squeezing her neck so she couldn't scream as he dragged her around behind the house. She flailed and kicked; she tried to get some leverage with her shoulder to flip him but couldn't manage it. Instead of pulling at the arms around her neck her hand went to her sidearm, flipped the holster open and drew the gun intending to shoot him in the leg or anywhere she could. She had never drawn her gun on the job before but now certainly seemed like the time to do it. But the Brother released one of his arms and grabbed the gun, raised it and struck Jess on the head. She collapsed and he let her drop to the ground. While she was dazed he found rope and tied her hands and legs and gagged her with a scarf.

The back door of the house opened and the woman, Sister Judith, looked on shocked at what he had done. Red-faced with emotion, her shock became a shocked tirade.

"What have you done!" she shrieked. "What have you done! You can't do this! You can't kidnap a police officer! Don't you think they're going to come looking?" Her frantic appeal fell on deaf ears.

"Shut up, woman! Get inside! I'll take care of this!"

"Like you take care of everything?" she shouted followed by a slammed door.

The noises brought another woman to her doorway and a man dragging a hoe walked up from tending a field. A small child peaked around the corner of a house.

"Go back inside!" the Brother shouted. "This is none of your business!" Eyes turned away and a door slammed.

Jess remained limp with closed eyes and feigned unconsciousness.

Brother Jedidiah lifted her slack body under the arms, his breath coming heavily and dragged her to a nearby shed throwing her in and shutting the door. She heard him leave.

She waited. Minutes passed. Everything was silent. She wondered how long he would leave her there. What were his intentions? His reaction was extreme for an assault charge.

She still had her cell phone and radio if she could get to one of them but, bound hands, feet and a mouth gag left her helpless. She struggled against the bindings and felt no give in them.

Then, the door opened. A small girl stood there framed by the sun behind her. She stared and Jess stared back, her heart tripped and she expected Jedidiah to appear at any second. She was a child about eight years of age in a shapeless blue dress and sweater. Her hair hadn't been combed today.

Jess struggled against the ropes and garbled grunts came out of her mouth. The child stood still, frightened and puzzled. Finally she spoke.

"Why are you tied up?" She hadn't advanced into the room. The door remained ajar. More grunts from Jess. The child came closer planting each step with a deliberate slowness, taking a measure of the situation. Finally, she sat down cross-legged beside Jess.

"Why are you tied up?"

Jess nudged her chin to indicate the gag and the girl reached with tentative fingers to remove it. "A man is trying to frighten me. It's working. It's kind of like a game. Can you help me? I need to get my hands free. If I get free the girls will win the game."

A grin creased the girl's face and she leaned forward. Her small hands worked at the binding and loosened it enough for Jess to finish the job.

"Thanks. I really needed that help to win." The child's face brightened into a wide smile.

Jess turned on her radio to broadcast her location and situation. It crackled but found the range and Jess was able to relate her situation. She let them know the subject's license plate number and that he should be considered armed and dangerous, "because," she added sheepishly, "he has my gun." They told her to stay put and out of sight.

That done, she considered the situation of the little girl. This was dangerous for her too and she had to find a way to protect her.

"This is a game?" the girl asked. "I thought you were here because of Charity."

"Charity?"

"Yes. He buried her. In the woods."

"Who did this?"

"Brother Jedidiah."

"How do you know?"

"I saw him." Jess caught her breath.

"What's your name? I'm Jessica."

"Verity."

"We met a few years ago," Jess said. "I remember you with Charity." They were still in the shed. Jess had released her legs and she knew help was on the way. "What did you see?"

"Charity was scared, screaming." Her voice dropped to a whisper. "Brother Jedidiah tried to, uh… uh, do sex with her and she hit him." Verity stopped and swallowed. She gathered her thoughts. "Then, he hit her and she went all quiet."

"What did he do then?" Jess kept an eye on the open door.

"He put her in a wheelbarrow and buried her in the woods."

This was horrific. It would devastate Zander Nilsson. He had been right to worry but wrong not to tell authorities. Not that the outcome would have been different, but he'll feel guilty that he doubted Charity's love.

Was the Brother good for Aimée Chandler too? Which burial did Carl Thurlow see?

"You remember it very clearly," Jess said gently. "You were smaller then."

Verity nodded. "I saw it. It was a bad thing."

"Yes, it was. Did you tell anyone?"

"My mother, Sister Sarah."

"What did she say?"

"That I shouldn't tell stories. That Brother Jedidiah was a good person. I didn't believe her."

"You were right, he's not. But, now that I am loose we can win the game and do something about Brother Jedidiah so he doesn't hurt anyone else." She gathered Verity into a hug. Her heart leaped as she heard sirens getting closer.

"Stay back," Jess told Verity. "Stay away from the door." Car doors slammed and a bullhorn called Brother Jedidiah to come out. Sturgis used his legal name.

"Jorden Markel, we know you are in there. Throw out the gun and come out with your hands up."

Jess risked a look out the shed door and saw a fleet of RCMP vehicles, bar-lights flashing, descend on the commune. They flanked the yard in front of the Brother's house, marksmen taking positions behind the cars.

"Jorden Markel. You have no chance. Give yourself up."

The standoff lasted only five minutes. She could picture Markel inside turning in circles trying to figure a way out when there wasn't one. Slowly the door to the house opened and Markel appeared holding his wife in front of him in a headlock to take the bullets if anyone decided to fire. His other arm was raised in the air with the gun in hand.

"Throw the gun down! Throw the gun down!"

Markel dropped the gun. "Kick it away! Now!" Markel complied.

"Let her go, Markel. Nobody's going to fire. We want a peaceful end to this." Reluctantly, Markel let the woman go and raised his hands. Officers swooped in, picked up the gun and cuffed him. They searched them both for weapons then bundled the weeping woman into a squad car. Markel went into a van.

Sturgis was on the horn again. "Morell! Come out if you can. The team is securing the area." Within minutes Jess came around the corner of the house holding the hand of a little girl. A trail of blood streaked her cheek where Jedidiah had hit her.

Sturgis walked to her. "Are you alright, Morell?"

"Yeah, I'm fine. This is Verity and she's a hero. She has a story to tell you."

"I'm glad you're okay, Morell, because there's a little matter of you disobeying an order and your weapon ending up in the hands of a murder suspect."

"There'll be paperwork," Jess said screwing up her face.

"Oh, at the very least," Sturgis replied resigned to it. "At the very least."

Todd Henley in civvies and his own car sat across the street from the Days Inn watching the building occupied by Adam Chandler. Todd was just guessing that he was there as he had no car to announce his location, but he'd gone there after his interview at the detachment. Todd figured he had to go out soon for food and he'd be right on his tail.

Henley was patient. In the two hours of waiting before Adam Chandler exited the inn and walked along Cranbrook Street, Todd drank steadily from the bottle of rye on the seat beside him. Todd's anger, now fueled by alcohol, provided all kinds of courage. All cleaned up as he was, Chandler looked less the bushman and more the doctor he had been. That less brawny look added to the confidence level Todd needed to accomplish his mission.

Chandler didn't act like he had a destination in mind, walking slowly and showing interest in the shops along the street. Todd followed him some distance and, when Chandler entered a convenience store, he parked his car and waited. After a few minutes Chandler exited the store with parcels in hand and walked back the way he had come. Todd turned the car around and followed his prey. It looked like Chandler was headed back to the inn. If he didn't act soon he would be out of luck.

Chandler entered the inn and Todd scrambled to catch up. Chandler took stairs to the second level, stopped at a room and inserted the key card. As Chandler opened the door, Henley swiftly filled the doorway behind him and grabbed Chandler around the neck in a choke-hold.

"Leave her alone," he ground out, spittle spraying Chandler's ear. "She belongs to me." He tightened his head-lock and punched Chandler hard around the head. Chandler elbowed Henley in the gut and twisted from his grip. He got in a punch to Henley's mid-section before being hit again and falling to the floor on his back. Chandler managed a hard kick at Henley, whose reflexes were dulled, and caught him in the crotch. Henley, his balls electrified by the kick, fell in a gasping, moaning heap with purple face and writhing in pain.

Lying on his back and breathing heavily, blood oozing from his nose and lip, Adam Chandler said, "If you mean Jess, she doesn't belong to anyone." He stared at Henley, recognized the cop. "You asshole. You just finished your career."

Henley's breathing returned to normal. "I fought for her and she was mine. You ruined everything I had."

"Not quite. You just finished whatever you had left." His nose was clogged with blood and his voice congested. He crawled to standing and reached the hotel phone. Punching in an outside line, he called nine-one-one.

CHAPTER 19

THE DETACHMENT BUZZED WITH THE excitement of the standoff at Charlotte Ridge. Sturgis told Jess she could go home and rest. She could come back for her statement after she'd collected herself. They also needed to talk about the stupidity of going to a suspect's home alone and the necessary investigation into her service weapon ending up in someone else's possession.

"I'm too wired to rest right now. Really, I need to be here. Just get me a cup of coffee and I'll make my statement now. And I want to make sure that little girl is alright"

"Her mother's here but we've called for a social worker to come and take charge. She'll sit in on the interview and make sure her home is safe for her to go back to. Why don't you go to the break room for a while?"

"Can't I sit in on Jorden Markel's interview?"

"No, of course not. You're a witness in this case. I can't let you anywhere near him."

"Do you think he's good for the Dr. Aimée murder?"

"We'll see won't we?"

As Jess was making her way to the break room, two constables came into the station with Todd Henley in handcuffs.

"What the...?" Jess's mouth fell open in disbelief. "What's going on? Todd?"

"He's in for assault." Everyone knew Jess and Todd had been a couple. "Sorry, Jess. He's in deep shit," the officer said.

"Who'd he assault? Why?" Jess genuinely puzzled as Todd stood with his head down.

"Adam Chandler. We dropped him at the ER. He probably needs a couple of stiches and his nose straightened. Todd said he was fighting for you." The officer almost smirked. "A bit Lancelet and King Arthur don't you think?"

"Idiot," Jess said. He didn't know if she meant him or Henley. Jess punched at Todd's shoulder. "Look at me," she said forcefully. Todd looked up. "You're a fucking idiot," she said into his face.

"Please, Jess," Todd said with raw pleading eyes.

She shook her head and left them, hurrying to a car. She needed to see Adam in the ER. She found him easily on a gurney, getting his bloody face cleaned by a nurse.

"We're really happy to see Dr. Chandler again but, not like this," the nurse said wiping gently at the blood.

"Jess, this is Janine, one of the best ER nurses in

Cranbrook." The slim nurse had dark hair and doe-in-the-headlights brown eyes.

"Hi, Janine." She glanced Janine's way then honed in on Adam. "Oh, Adam, you look like you've been in the wars. I'm so sorry Todd is such a jerk."

"I'm sorry, too. He obviously thinks you're his property. Not the best way to hold an independent and competent woman like you."

"You know me better in three weeks than he does in three years." She smiled and held his hand. "You know, for a while I had breather phone calls and I felt like someone was watching me. For a while I considered Todd for it. This makes me wonder if it really was him. He's worse than a jerk."

"You really think he'd do that?"

"I found him one time in the spot the prowler voyeur would stand. He had an excuse for being there but I certainly started to wonder."

"I think I'll leave you two for a few minutes," Janine said with a smile. As she leaned across Adam to collect soiled towels, a gold locket she was wearing slipped out from the neck of her scrubs into Adam's line of vision. Reacting swiftly he grabbed the locket holding the chain tightly.

"What the hell? Where did you get this? Where?" He pulled on the chain.

"Stop! You're hurting me." The nurse grabbed at Adam's hand to release his hold. She stepped back clinging to the locket, her face twisted in shock.

"Adam! What's going on? What's with the locket?" Jess said.

"It's Aimée's! It's hers! I know it!"

"Okay, okay." Jess said grabbing his shoulders. "How do you know?"

"I gave it to her, when she graduated from med school. She never took it off!"

"Janine, where did you get it?" Jess leaned over Adam. "Let me see it," she said reaching out her hand, the weight of her uniform demanding action.

"My boyfriend gave it to me," Janine said tearfully. "It was in a velvet box and everything."

She placed the locket in Jess's hand. Holding the locket by the chain, Jess examined it for markings. It was a gold oval with fine etchings on the front. There was no inscription. "It's not engraved," she said.

"But there's a tiny scratch on the back at the bottom. A dog did it when he jumped up. We were going to put her graduation date on the back. We just never got around to it. Where did you get it?" Anger, stress, puzzlement played across his face.

"Who's your boyfriend?" Jess said with a tone of urgent authority. She was looking for the scratch.

Janine pressed her lips into a tight line.

Jess tried softer encouragement. "I've found the scratch, Janine. C'mon. I don't care that you have it; just say the name."

Her eyes teared. "He's… married. I don't want to get him in trouble."

"Nothing will happen to you if you tell me who. I want the truth."

Her face set into a blank stare. "Michael Heath. He gave it to me." With the telling she couldn't hold it together any longer and dissolved into earnest crying. "How did this happen? I didn't know it was Aimée's. I didn't know!"

"Okay, Janine. We just have to get to the bottom of this. Here," Jess said, "get me an envelope to put this in. It's evidence." Turning to Adam she said, "I'll be right back. This could be our break. I have to notify Staff Sergeant Sturgis."

Jess went outside to make the call. "This could be it," she told Sturgis.

"Come back to the barn. I want two squad cars to pick him up. His wife in one and Heath in the other. No talking between them."

"Got it."

She went back to Adam's side. "Gotta go. I'll let you know what happens but, Heath is in for some serious questioning."

She picked up Franks at the detachment and realized she no longer had a gun. It was locked up in the Exhibit Vault. She went to Sturgis.

"I'll let you have Henley's for now until we can get another from stores. He won't be using it." He gave her a stare as if daring her to lose possession of this one too.

With a second car with two officers following, they drove to Charlotte Ridge and into Heath's yard. He was working on the porch, a hammer in hand. On seeing the cars and four officers he threw down the hammer and shouted, "No! This isn't going to happen!" He was inside his house in a second and Jess heard the dead bolt thrown.

"No, Michael! Don't!" could be heard from inside. "He's got a gun!" Eva Heath shouted.

"Shut up, shut up!" Then a cry of pain.

"Heath!" Jess called. "Don't do this. We want to talk to you and we can do this simply and easily."

"No we can't. This isn't simple or easy. You're going to have to work for it." The sound of breaking glass and a rifle barrel appeared in the window. The officers took positions behind the cars, weapons pulled. Jess's line of vision was directly on Heath.

"Heath, this isn't necessary. Throw down your gun and come out, now."

In response, Heath fired a round into one of the cars. Then a second. There was no hesitation; Jess pulled her gun.

"If you have a shot, take it!" Jess called out. Heath rose into the window a bit too far. Jess aimed and fired. A cry of pain and he dropped from sight. "Hold your fire." All was silence.

"Mrs. Heath, throw the gun out and come out with your hands up. Nobody's going to hurt you."

They waited a minute and the door opened a crack. She threw the rifle into the yard.

"Is there anyone else in the house? Are there any more weapons?"

"No! You've got to help Michael. He's bleeding

bad!" She appeared in the doorway hands high, visibly shaking and close to hysteria. "Cuff her," she said. Eva Heath blubbered as she was cuffed.

Jess swung the door open and slowly rounded the corner of the room where Heath lay bleeding. Two officers came in behind her, guns drawn, and started searching the house. Jess scanned the immediate area and, finding it safe, dropped beside Heath. He was breathing noisily and blood poured from his neck. She grabbed an afghan off the couch and pressed it to the wound. Heath moaned and opened his eyes.

"It didn't have to be this way, Heath. Why? Why?"

"Of course, it did." He choked on blood that gurgled from his throat. "She ruined our family. This was the only way."

"Why did you lead us to the body? Why?"

"There had to be an end to the story, hadn't there?"

He tried to say more as his head dropped to the side and he stopped breathing. Jess sat cross-legged beside him and tried to fathom the path to self-destruction that Heath had chosen.

She ruined our family.

Jess heard the crackle of the radio as Franks directed the ambulance and the rest of their team to their location. She heard Eva Heath keening in the back of the squad car. Jess sat there not moving. It would be a while before she moved.

CHAPTER 20

"I TOLD YOU TO TAKE A week, Jess," Sturgis stood over her while she sat at a desk in the detachment. She was in civvies and not really doing anything.

"I'm not doing anything, sir." The spring that was wound so tight inside Jess since the shooting was starting to uncoil.

"That's the way it should be, only not doing it at home." His stern look made Jess stand up.

"Okay. I'm just interested in how everything is playing out. What you found at Heath's."

"Come into my office and I'll give you a rundown, then, you go home." They closed the door behind them and Jess sat in the chair opposite Sturgis's desk.

"First, his vehicle matches the forensics we have. And he smokes the same brand of cigarette butts found at the site. Also Keith Rymes says he did body work on Heath's SUV. He's searching for the paperwork."

"A good start," Jess said.

"It gets better. He was a writer, right? So he wrote it all down. Wrote it up like the plot of a book."

"No way! How did it start?"

Sturgis gathered his thoughts. "Several years ago Heath's daughter, Amanda, lost her own daughter, three-year-old Wendy, to the courts. She was taken away on the testimony of Dr. Aimée-Marie Chandler and put into foster care. About a year after that, Heath's daughter, Amanda, died of a heroin overdose. Heath nursed his anger for years. It's all over his writing that Aimée Chandler ruined his family. Then one night after he'd been drinking in a pub, he fell asleep in his car in the pub parking lot. When he woke up it was three a.m., raining hard and he started home. He saw Dr. Chandler on the roadside, standing out of her car and doing something to the windshield wipers. He was still drunk and his anger at her surfaced and he plowed into her. He decided to hide her body."

"What happened to the car?"

"He used his car to push it over the cliff."

"And we couldn't see it."

"Nope. If he had lived and could tell us the general area, maybe we'd find it but not likely now."

"Did his wife know about it?"

"Doesn't seem that way."

"But he wrote it all down."

"Yes, almost like a novel, even divided into chapters except he didn't change the names. The last line in every chapter was 'She ruined our family.' He was reliving it every time he opened the file. It's all on his computer."

"Why did he insert himself into the murder by taking us to the grave?"

"Just his way of furthering his story. He wanted an ending. It probably would have been his next novel."

"He visited the site often, didn't he? All those cigarette butts."

"Couldn't stay away. Murderers often revisit the site."

"Poor Aimée Chandler." Jess sighed deeply. "Poor Adam." A pause. "And the commune death? And what about Todd?"

"Todd is on suspension and is charged with assault. He'll lose his job if convicted and will probably do time."

"I think he stalked me a couple of years ago and made breather phone calls."

Sturgis sat up straight. "Why didn't you say something?"

"There wasn't any way to say for sure unless he confesses to it."

"You can bet we'll be asking," Sturgis said determinedly.

"As for the commune, Jorden Markel has been charged with first degree murder. There is also an assault charge against him for what he did to you. The child and Carl Thurlow are witnesses—not that Carl would hold up well in court—and his wife, Sister Judith, knew about the murder from Verity. Besides, there were some rags in the grave that had to have been used by the killer, probably for cleaning up blood. We're tracing the DNA now. We're hoping for DNA on the wheelbarrow but that's a long shot. We're talking to all the other residents there and we're building a case."

"I'd like to be in on all this," Jess said hopefully.

"Not on the Markel case, of course. You're a witness. But later you'll be part of the Heath case. But, not till you're cleared by a psychologist. Take some break time. Go canoeing and clear your mind."

"First I have a funeral to attend."

"Aimée Chandler?"

"Yeah. It's this afternoon."

"I'm glad it's over for all of them."

"So am I."

Jess left and went home to change into a dress appropriate for a funeral. She arrived as the short memorial service started. The chapel was full. Jess recognized many of the people present as doctors and hospital staff. Adam delivered a thoughtful, sensitive eulogy followed by comments by her friends. A reception room provided beverages and snacks. Adam was kept busy talking and introducing Aimée's parents and brother to her many friends. Finally, he had a few moments for Jess. He'd bought a new suit for the occasion. His face still held some bruises.

"I'm so glad to see you," he said warmly taking her hand.

"I'm glad it's over."

"Sturgis had me into the office yesterday and told me the story. Almost literally a story. I'm glad Heath kept such detailed notes. They might never have put it together." He took a breath. "I was hoping to see you at the detachment. Are you avoiding me?"

"No! Not at all. I've had some enforced time off, that's all. After an officer-involved-shooting, you know. They want me to take some time before I go back to work."

He looked at her thoughtfully. "I can think of a restful place to do that."

"I can too," she answered, eyes gleaming.

"Will you come? And stay for a while?" There was hope in his voice.

"When?"

"I have to see Kelly and Meena and Derrick, Aimée's parents and brother, off at the airport tomorrow. What about after that?"

"I'll be ready by mid-afternoon. I'll pick you up."

He squeezed her hands and moved on to talk to someone else. As she left the reception her mind was already on high-end camping and the man that went with it.

At home, she started a small pile in her living room, sleeping bag, pillow. Adam would have the necessities but she added a bottle of wine, then, a second. She slipped into a hot tub, shaved her legs and soaked, finishing with body lotion over her entire body. Maybe she would dream tonight.

The next day dragged and she filled it as best she could with household chores. But, finally, she picked up Adam at the Days Inn. He looked marvelous to her, strong and fresh in his new jeans and trimmed beard, happy and confident that the future would be better than the past. She thought his smile could rival the sun.

She thought about the cabin in the woods, of the man who filled the space. She wanted that man, that home. That was it exactly. They'd never even kissed but she knew she was going home.

Adam took the passenger seat in the car. With key in hand, Jess looked at him and said, "Okay. Here's the deal. I'm not starting this car until you tell me about the pristine quilt in your cabin."

Adam threw back his head in a hearty laugh that came out as more like a hoot. "That's what's on your mind? That's what you want to know?"

She nodded clasping the key firmly, a glint in her eye.

With a broad smile he said, "Okay. Here's the thing…"